CW00395077

# CRIMINAL CONDUCT

## ROBERT ULPH

To: R Evil O, Tinki, Goji, and the Homies in Hampshire

Cover Image: Bielloriehppe and Rapadalen as seen from the location of Noel's campsite on Låddebákte, by the author.

© 2021 Robert Ulph All rights reserved. No part of this publication may be reproduced or used in any form without express permission of the author.

## Preface

This book is a work of fiction. All the names of individuals (other than John Maynard Keynes), characters, events and incidents in this book are either the product of the author's imagination or used in a fictitious manner. The only exceptions are certain of the historical details relating to the Coronavirus pandemic which began in 2020, and details of certain UK legislation. Any other resemblance to actual persons, living or dead, or actual events is purely coincidental.

The author also does not condone any acts of violence or intimidation of the types depicted in this book, whether authorised or unauthorised.

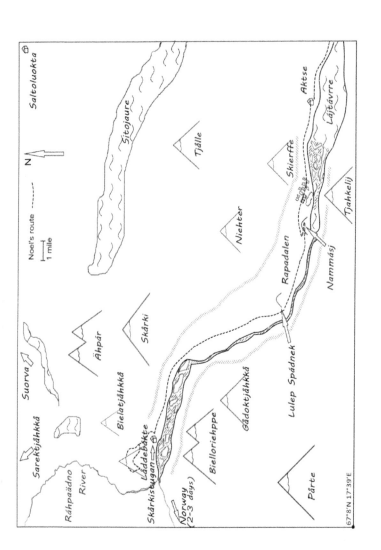

Schematic map of the mountains and other locations referred to in the book

## Tuesday, 26th September

If we travel to a remote destination to take a break from our everyday life, is that good in that it gives us perspective on things back home? Or is it bad, in that we are perhaps running away from our problems? Might our problems simply come with us? Noel McVay had travelled from London for a small adventure in Sweden, and was about to find out.

Noel was going to undertake a ten-day solo hike in the mountains of the Sarek National Park, beyond the Arctic Circle. Over the preceding 36 hours he had flown from London to Stockholm's Arlanda Airport, had then taken an overnight train to the northern iron ore mining town of Gällivare, then a bus to the town of Jokkmokk, a taxi to the start of the trail, and walked ten miles along the northern shores of two lakes, Tjaktjajávrre and Lájtávrre, to reach his present campsite. His campsite was in a small clearing, not far from the small collection of buildings at Aktse, just outside the National Park. Sarek is a great wilderness area of mountains, glaciers and deep valleys, extending to the west from Aktse. It was a destination he had always wanted to visit, famed as it was for its beautiful scenery. It was good to be away from home, although in his head he was still more back home than in the Arctic.

Aktse lies just below the beautiful Ráhpaädno delta, and is an access point for Sarek. Noel had come in September, relatively late in the season. It had been something of a last-minute decision, but it was also a good time to be here. Firstly, there should be no mosquitoes. The clouds of mosquitoes in Arctic Sweden in summer can make life an absolute misery, their numbers almost unimaginable if you have not experienced them before. Also, the colours of the trees would be at their most beautiful now; beautiful golden browns everywhere. The weather would be colder than at the height of summer, and snow was a possibility, but it was unlikely to be really cold.

It was only 9pm, but Noel was ready for bed – he hadn't been able to sleep that well on the train the night before. He got up, and out of his small, one-man tent. He washed his hands, which were sticky from extracting his dinner from the depths of the foil bag in which he had rehydrated it with just a spoon, and cleaned his teeth. He emptied out the remains of his dinner onto the ground, as he hadn't been able to finish it.  He got back into his tent and into his sleeping bag. He folded up his fleece jacket to make a pillow, turned off his torch, set an alarm on his phone, and started to doze off.

As Noel lay there, a rustling sound outside the tent disturbed him. He heard it again. It exhaled sharply. It sounded like an animal had come for the vegetable couscous that he hadn't been able to finish. It was a little bit uncomfortable lying there with this animal so close. So he grabbed his headtorch, and jumped out of his sleeping bag to open up the front of his tent as fast as he could. He saw the rear of an animal as it ran off. A small deer, probably a roe deer. Fair enough, let it come back for the rest of my dinner, he thought to himself. Now that he knew that the animal wasn't anything threatening he would feel more comfortable if it returned, and would be better able to get to sleep.

*

## Wednesday 27th September

Noel woke up. He checked the time on his phone – it was not yet 7a.m., and his alarm clock had not gone off. He was surprised to find himself awake at this time, given that it would not even be six o'clock back in the UK. It was getting light. Noel knew that he would only have eleven hours of daylight to make use of, so he decided to get up right then. He got dressed, put his boots on, and went outside to sort out some breakfast.

Outside, Noel could see through the trees that it was in fact reasonably light, and that it was rather cloudy. There wasn't much of last night's dinner left on the ground; it looked as if the deer must have returned to finish it off. He put the stove on to boil up some water for breakfast, and washed his face. Once the water had boiled he poured most of it in for another boil-in-the-bag meal, "Hot Cereal with Raspberries". He made a coffee, and retreated into his tent. He noticed to his disappointment that it was raining slightly.

Noel's plan for the first full day of his hike was to follow a trail for a short distance to the north, and then cut off left over open ground towards the summit of Skierffe, a total climb of about 700 metres. Skierffe lies immediately north of the Ráhpaädno delta, and offers a fantastic view over it, with a sheer drop right down to it. It is as if the former glacier had simply sheared off the face of the mountain. From Skierffe he would carry on up the valley a little before dropping down through the forest to approach the hill known as "Nammásj". This sits, somewhat improbably, in the centre of the valley. He planned to camp for the night on top of Nammásj. He was a little apprehensive about cutting through the forest; he knew it would be hard work, with no path, but the distance was less than a mile and he was sure that somehow or other he would make it through.

The inclement weather made Noel change his mind. The approach to Skierffe would be very exposed, and not very enjoyable in this weather, so instead he would stay in the valley. Further up the valley, beyond Nammásj there is a footpath and this is typically approached by boat from Aktse, through the delta. But Noel knew that this boat service would have stopped back in August once the water level got too low for the boat to run through the delta. With the refuge at Aktse now closed, Noel knew that his chances of getting a boat were non-existent. So what Noel would do would be to walk through the forest towards the base of Skierffe, then over the boulder field at its base, and then on through more forest to the base of Nammásj, and up from there. So much forest might be a bit of a slog, but he would be a lot more sheltered.

Again, Noel couldn't finish his meal. He had been eating a lot to bulk up before the trip so perhaps it was understandable that his appetite wasn't that great. Once he got going and was expending more calories it would certainly improve.

Noel packed up his sleeping bag and mat, packed his rucksack, put his boots on, went outside, took his tent down, brushed his teeth, hoped that his night-time companion in the campsite also liked raspberry breakfast cereal, and set off to walk the short distance into the clearing where the scattered huts of Aktse were located. His fully loaded rucksack weight close to 30kg. As he was walking, he noticed from the tops of the trees that there was something of a breeze blowing.

Noel arrived at Aktse. It seemed to be completely deserted. From here, he had a better view of his surroundings; he could see the summit of Skierffe, and across the delta he could see Tjahkelij, a mountain of similar height to Skierffe, but longer. It also had a steep face down to the delta, although nothing like as sheer as that of Skierffe. Tjahkelij's summit was largely in cloud and it looked as if there was some fresh snow up there.

Noel got his map out again and spread it over a picnic table to get an overview of his planned route. To his surprise, a door of one of the huts opened, and a man started walking down the wooden steps leading from the front of it. OK, so there was someone still around. The man was probably in his 60s, and Noel guessed that he was probably responsible for running the hut.

4

"God morgon! Can I help?" asked the man.

"Ah hello," replied Noel, sounding slightly surprised. "I wasn't expecting to see anyone here."

"Well, as you probably know the cabins are closed now. But I am here for a few days more just to tidy up things now that the season has ended."

"I see. I'm intending to spend a few days hiking up Rapadalen and then out of the park to the north."

"You are quite late" replied the man. "But actually it is a good time to go. The valley is at its most beautiful at this time of year, and all the animals are busy eating to prepare for winter, so you may see some wildlife. Do you have an emergency locator beacon with you?"

"Yes, I do," replied Noel, showing the man through the pocket of his jacket the device which he was carrying to trigger a rescue service in the event of an accident.

"Ah, you should be fine," replied the man. "How many days are you going for?"

"Ten days. I'm planning to walk up and out at Suorva, not going too fast, just taking my time."

The man gave Noel some advice on the best approach to Nammásj, given that Noel would be passing below the base of Skierffe without much of a path, and then returned to his hut. He came out a few minutes later carrying an urn of lingonberry tea for Noel to help himself to. The man went back inside and Noel sat consuming some tea, while continuing to mull over his route. It was going to be quite a slog for a first day, but if he could reach Nammásj, and camp on the top tonight, that would be magnificent.

Noel finished his tea, put his cup away, and took off some layers of clothing. It immediately left him feeling cold, but over the years he had learnt to wear fewer clothes than seemed necessary when setting off. Carrying a heavy rucksack entailed burning a lot of calories and generating a lot of heat. Noel knew that if he felt comfortable when he set off, he would be stopping within fifteen minutes to remove some layers. He hauled his rucksack onto his back, groaning a bit at the weight of it. But he knew that he had successfully managed similar weights before. And of course the weight would go down over the course of the hike as he ate his food. He set off up the valley, through the clearing at Aktse, past some very neat clapboard houses. They were decorated with reindeer antlers and, he noted, one moose's antler. Rapadalen is famous for its very large moose, supposedly the largest in Sweden. With luck, Noel would see some. The path that he was on was taking him down to the lake, to the jetty for the boat service, and he didn't want to go there. So, at a point, where there was something of a path off into the forest, he plunged into the trees.

Noel followed the path for a bit, unsure of how well it would serve him. After a while it started to peter out. He followed it for a bit, lost it, returned to look for it, followed it a bit, and then lost it again. He decided that it wasn't worth continuing to go back to look for it, as the ground through the trees was reasonably clear, and all he had to do was keep going in the same direction. He simply had to make sure that he stayed between the mountainside to his right and the lake and channels of the delta to his left.

So Noel carried on. Whereas where he had camped last night he was amongst pine trees, now the forest he was in consisted largely of birch trees. He was unlikely to see any more pine trees now until the very end of the hike. They grow at lower altitudes than the birch. Given the time of year, the leaves of the birch trees had all turned a golden-brown colour, and many of them had already fallen.  Whenever there was a slight gust of wind there would be a shower of further leaves falling, like glitter in a snowdome. It was quite pleasant to be walking through this, and also to be getting some fresh air after being in London for so long. As he hiked, on several occasions, woodcock flew up from under his feet and gave him a start. They always flew off to disappear again, in silence, but their outline with the long bill was unmistakeable.

Noel carried on walking through the forest. Mostly it was rather quiet, with some sound from the wind in the treetops. He found no further sign of any path, and had to navigate past quite a few boulders, fallen trees and assorted hollows in the ground. But he didn't mind the slow progress that much, he did not have a lot of distance to cover that day. He had a compass on his watch that enabled him to follow what he assumed must be a fairly direct route.

Noel enjoyed the opportunity to spend some time alone in his head. He thought about how he found the Swedes he met, such as the man at the huts, to be friendly and welcoming. They were always so happy to speak English, which they invariably spoke very well. He tried to think of how many words of Swedish he knew.  There was "hej" (hi), "Skål" (cheers), and "tack" (thank you). That was about it. Oh, also "fjällpipare", a word he had picked up on a previous trip, being Swedish for a bird, the dotterel, which breeds on the high fells. It seemed a very nice word, that must have been why it had stuck in his mind. "Cheers, hello dotterel, thank you." That was his limit. If it takes a knowledge of 20,000 words to be fluent in a language, that meant he had 19,996 words to go. It's going to be quite a job, he thought. He was considering that he might have to learn Swedish after the hike was over.

After about an hour and a half, Noel began to have clear views of the summit of Skierffe, high up above him to his right, although it was partly in cloud. In another half an hour he was out of the forest, and faced with a long stretch of huge boulders in front of him. This was the talus field of Skierffe, rocks that had fallen down over millennia from Skierffe's face. Not far away, and to his left, there was a small lake, the boulders stretching out into it. He decided to sit down on a rock for a break. He took off his rucksack, brushed out bits of tree that had got caught up in it (and in his hair), and thought about his next steps.

Noel looked up at the huge face of Skierffe that now towered above him, and took a moment to imagine the vast glacier that must have flowed right where he was sitting, probably until about 10,000 years ago. Skierffe and Tjahkelij must have formed a very well-defined channel for it to flow through. He thought back to learning at school all about the multitude of different glacial land features. Terminal and lateral and medial moraines. U-shaped and hanging valleys. Drumlins and eskers. Corries, cirques and cwms. Ah, of course, there was another word of Swedish that Noel knew. Smorgasbord. There was a smorgasbord of different glaciological shapes and forms. That made five words now. He reflected on how glacial land forms were so eagerly taught in schools, yet knowledge of them was seemingly of such limited use to most people.

You could look at the very existence of glaciers as curious, Noel thought, because surely they didn't have to be here on our planet. In order that there would be life on earth to ask the question of the need for glaciers, the world needed seas to hold water, volcanoes to create land, a sun to provide energy and to move the water from the seas onto the land via clouds. It needed a magnetic field to protect the earth from dangerous radiation. But it really didn't need glaciers. Rivers alone would have done all that was needed in terms of carrying sediment down to the valleys where life could prosper. So why were glaciers here? Was it just by accident?

Clearly it was natural that the world should seem to be nicely designed to fit the needs of supporting life. Noel was not religious, but if the world had been created by God, it was natural that God would have created it as a good fit for our needs. But equally if it had been created purely by scientific processes, it should be a good fit for our needs because there was a selective bias – Noel wouldn't be now finding himself on a planet and pondering these questions if the planet didn't suit the needs of life. Either way it was inevitable that our planet should look a good fit for meeting the needs of supporting life.

But why glaciers? Were they here just here by chance? Simply an added feature of the world that happened to exist? Maybe, thought Noel. Just maybe. But what about the idea that God, on finishing his Creation, sat back, quite satisfied, and decided to polish the product up a bit and add some finishing touches. So He included glaciers as an optional extra. Maybe to give geography teachers something to teach.

Taking his camera out, Noel took a few photos and hauled his rucksack back onto his back. The next section was somewhat daunting. He had a long stretch ahead of him to make his way across the boulders in the talus slope. Some of them were enormous, the size of houses. If one came down right now that could be the end for Noel. But the chance was not very high. There were small trees between the boulders and moss growing on them, so they had clearly been there for some time, and were not falling at a great rate.

Noel set off, heaving and hauling himself across the boulders. It was far from easy with a heavy rucksack on. He needed full use of his hands to climb over the rocks. The small trees that were there got in the way whenever he had to drop down, although at times they were also of use as holds for him to climb back up. The rocks themselves were quite slippery, so he had to pay full attention to not fall and hurt himself. He couldn't head further away from the cliff as he was hemmed in on that side by quite a sizeable lake. He could see quite a number of whooper swans sitting scattered across the lake. They eyed him warily as he moved along the boulder field, swimming away as he got closer, but not flying. In a few weeks' time they would all be gone, maybe to overwinter in Britain.

Noel made steady, but inevitably slow, progress over the boulder field. It was quite a struggle, and he really longed to be at the other side. But he broke the distance down in his head into 100 metre units to make it more manageable. The whole distance he needed to cover was probably about 600 metres. In good British style Noel switched between metric and imperial units depending on the nature of the object being measured. Inches and feet for short lengths, metres for middling distances (because he could easily visualise 100 metres from the school running track, but he wasn't so sure about yards), and miles for longer distances (because that was what a car's milometer told him). For temperatures he used Centigrade for low temperatures (what was notable about a temperature of 25 degrees Fahrenheit?) and Fahrenheit for high temperatures (80 degrees Fahrenheit sounds hot, 27 degrees Centigrade doesn't particularly). It never seemed to cause any problems, but Noel imagined that it must be a uniquely British approach.

As Noel approached the far side of the boulder field, he decided that it was time for lunch. He would take it sitting on a rock, rather than in the forest ahead, so as to have better views. He had some reasonably fresh food with him – some bread, ham and cheese from the store in Jokkmokk, and some crisps and a cereal bar from back home. It was still raining a bit, so he put his fleece on under his waterproof jacket. Once he had finished eating, Noel got out his binoculars and scanned the view ahead to Nammásj, by now clearly visible ahead of him. It was only a mile and a half away but the terrain in between Noel and it was carpeted with trees. There was something otherworldly about it, sitting as it was in the middle of the valley. Normally mountains don't occur in valleys. There had to be something special about it, for it not to have been worn away by the glaciers that would have enveloped it in the Ice Ages.

It would not be possible to climb Nammásj directly as the near side was essentially a cliff. Noel would need to go around to the rear of it, still through the trees, in order to approach it from the more gentle, western slope. As he scanned the hill, a large falcon, probably a goshawk, was soaring high up between him and Nammásj. He was getting the impression that, although the valley seemed rather quiet, there was actually quite a lot living here, and probably much of it unseen by him.

By the time he had finished looking around and having lunch, it was 1:20 p.m. He was keen to get going. He still envisaged camping up on Nammásj, ideally to see both the tonight's sunset and tomorrow's sunrise from its summit. But first he needed to get going through the second section of forest. As the man at Aktse had advised him, it would be necessary to carry plenty of water up onto the hill. There was little chance that there would be any sort of stream running down it. This meant that Noel needed to plan how he was going to stock up with water before he climbed. There was a significant stream marked on his map running down from the north, which he would have to cross and he was confident that that would serve his needs for collecting water.

Noel dropped down below the rock where he had been sitting. He needed to relieve himself and wanted to get out of the wind to do so. There was a large flat rock, and, to his surprise, a number of

11

old bones lying on it. They were quite large and curved and Noel assumed that they must be reindeer bones. Strange that a reindeer had died here, thought Noel. Perhaps the reindeer had found itself up against the boulder field when migrating down the valley for winter and not been able to get across. Or perhaps it had been going up the valley and had made it across the boulder field and then expired after the exertion, thought Noel. He would have had some sympathy.

Once he had finished relieving himself, Noel examined the reindeer bones. There were some antlers there as well. In turn he picked up three of them and threw each one as hard as he could out into the lake. He was still very weighed down by issues that he had at home, and this was a way to take his anger out on something.

Noel entered the forest again, and pressed on through it. The view to the sky was largely open, and so navigating towards Nammásj was not difficult. But the going now was definitely harder than it had been in the forest before the boulder field. There were occasional open meadows which Noel quickly found were too boggy to easily traverse. This caused him to head more to the right than he had intended, so slowing his progress towards Nammásj. Mentally it was quite draining because it felt so slow. There were so many fallen branches and boggy hollows that he had to navigate around that it would have been easy to lose motivation. But rather than focusing too much on his destination, Noel kept his thoughts in the moment at hand. He knew that he just had to keep going and he would get there, and he had enough time. So he simply kept pushing his way through the forest. At one moment, a willow grouse burst up in front of him and flew off, its white wings whirring at great speed, to land somewhere unseen.

Noel could see the western and northern faces of Nammásj as he skirted the mountain, all clearly too steep for him to take to reach the top. But he could see from his map, and knew from his prior reconnaissance on Google Earth back home, that the western side was much gentler. That was where he would climb. Nammásj has about 300m of altitude above the valley floor; really it's not much more than a hill.

As he started making progress around Nammásj Noel was mindful of his need to collect water for his night on top. He could see, up above him and to his right, the stream coming down, quite directly, from the mountain Niehter, which would provide him with his water. He could see where it fell through a waterfall at one point, embedded quite deeply in the steep side of the valley.

In due course Noel came upon the lower stretches of this same stream. It was running surprisingly clear, given the muddiness of the surrounding area of forest. Noel stopped, half-filled his water bottle, and drank it all, to ensure that he would be well hydrated from that point on. He then filled the bottle again, and also his cooking pot which had a tight-fitting lid. He inserted this into the bottom of his rucksack, under his sleeping bag, in such a way as he was reasonably confident it would stay horizontal while he walked on. The sleeping bag itself would be safe from any leaks. He kept it in a watertight bag. Getting his sleeping bag wet would be a calamity – he would then have no option but to sleep in all his clothes. That wouldn't be enough to keep him warm, so he would sleep very badly, and probably end up cutting the trip short by hiking straight out.

Noel crossed the stream without difficulty, and waded through the boggy field towards the trees on other side. Above him, the north-facing cliff of Nammásj was giving way to a scree. He could have climbed up that, but he knew it would be hard work, so he carried on round until he got onto the more gently sloping ground at the back of the mountain. Here the going, although uphill, was somewhat easier. For the first time, he got out his walking poles from his rucksack and used them so that his arms could do some of the work of getting him up the slope, not just his legs. The ground was drier and there was more space between the trees. He carried on, skirting around and up the mountain. Another willow grouse flew off. Noel pressed on, but he was starting to feel quite tired. Having to go uphill at the end of the day was tiring, and Noel's fitness now, at the beginning of the trip was perhaps not what it might be. He pushed on, over a small ridge, through some tight-packed trees and, suddenly, in front of him, bingo, there was a path! A really good path too. Noel stopped, resting much of his weight on his walking poles, and took some deep breaths. It was a big relief to be connected to the world again. The path that he had found runs up to Nammásj from off of the main path in Rapadalen. It wasn't marked on his map but he had been fairly confident that enough people would climb the mountain for there to be one. But it was a more substantial path than he had been expecting.

Noel took the path up towards the top of Nammásj. It was pleasant not to have to keep looking ahead and think about how he was going to get around whatever obstacle might lie ahead. The weather had improved, and both Skierffe and Tjakhelij were now out of the clouds. But it was still overcast and there was quite a breeze. It was 4:45pm. He was concerned about whether he was going to find somewhere to camp if he carried on right to the top. Any location needed not to be too exposed or rocky. But soon he came upon a spot that looked adequate, more or less out of the trees, but still such that there were enough trees around to give him some shelter. He decided that it would do for the night, and he offloaded his rucksack. He needed to put his tent up. But first he wanted to go and see the view from the summit, and he wanted to do this before it got dark. He put on some warmer clothes, got out his camera and binoculars, and hiked on up and over to the edge of the cliff, for a view over the delta.

The view, of course, was spectacular. Noel had looked at photos taken from the mountain before he left, and this was every bit as impressive. He could see the winding main channel of the Ráhpaädno as it passed through the delta, and numerous sizeable lakes on either side of the river, right up to the bases of Skierffe and Tjahkelij. The land between the water was a golden colour from the birch trees. There were islands in the river, flanked by trees and with further wetlands amidst them. With his binoculars Noel could make out the swans that he had passed earlier in the day, and could just make out the huts and clearing at Aktse. This is why he had come, and he at last felt that he had arrived at his destination. He stood up, mouth agape, and stretched his arms out, in an expression of awe at his surroundings. Or maybe he was just stretching his arms because his shoulders ached from carrying a heavy rucksack all day. Anyway, he felt the need to stretch his arms.

It was certainly a remarkable destination that Noel had chosen to visit. How did he know about it? Well, he had been hiking a little to the north of Sarek a year earlier, where he had climbed Kebnekaise, the highest mountain in Sweden. After he returned, further examination on Google Earth revealed an equally mountainous area to the south, which looked even more remote. Some of the photos of Rapadalen in particular looked magnificent. So he chose this for his next destination. He had posted about his plans on HikeBackCountry.com, an online hiking forum where he had got some useful information. One poster on there in particular, who went under the name "Tromso2000", had been extremely helpful. Tromso2000 had had a lot of experience of the area, and explained to Noel the best time to go, where to camp, how to provision himself for the trip, and, with Tromso2000's help, Noel was able to finalise his choice of route.

Tromso2000's enthusiasm for the location was very evident and Noel promised to tell him all about it after the trip was over.

Noel walked around to find a good place to sit to scan the delta more carefully. There was an area of flattened vegetation between some of the rocks. It was curious. Had someone been sitting there? Maybe. Perhaps there was someone else around. It didn't seem like a place that an animal would choose to rest. Oh well. He sat down for a bit and got his binoculars out to scan below. Surely somewhere down there in all that delta there had to be a moose, busily fattening itself up for winter? But he couldn't find one. He got up and walked over the rocks to the south side of the mountain. Here he had more views over the delta and across through a gap to the west of Tjahkelij, where he could see a long stretch of forest extending out to the horizon. He still couldn't shake off the depression that he felt about events back home, but being where he was did now feel uplifting. Noel walked back to where he had left his rucksack, carefully removed his pot of water (which thankfully seemed not to have leaked) and put up his tent. It was starting to get dark.

Putting on a down jacket, Noel rummaged in his rucksack, firstly for his headtorch, and secondly for dinner. Pasta Bolognese tonight! It was a bit of a lucky dip because he couldn't actually see what he was pulling out from the depths of his rucksack. He got out his stove, fuel and lighter, and took them over to some rocks nearby to start preparing his dinner. He needed the distance. A tent fire out here would be a very distressing situation. It was at this point that Noel realised that his plan for carrying water up the mountain wasn't without a flaw. He only needed a quarter of the water that he had carried in his cooking pot to prepare his dinner. But he had nowhere to put the surplus water while he prepared his dinner. He couldn't pour it away because he was going to need it in the morning. And he didn't want to boil it all as that would use up too much fuel. But there was a solution. Noel decided that he could forgive the manufacturers of his camping dinners for their excess packaging. He took out the pouch from yesterday's dinner, cleaned it out with a bit of moss and some water, rinsed it and poured most of the water from his pot into it, before sealing it up. It looked like storing the spare water in this way was going to work. Breakfast tomorrow might have a bit of a tang to it, though.

The pot boiled, Noel poured the water into his bag of pasta, stirred it, sealed it up and took it back to his tent. He needed to wait six minutes for it to rehydrate fully. So he sat back for a bit to look at his map. It was a relief to be in his tent at the end of the day, with some hot food. He noticed for the first time that his feet were aching. The day had been tiring, with the almost total lack of any paths, but he was satisfied with the progress that he had made. Outside the wind was still blowing somewhat and the remaining leaves on the trees were rustling, but he felt comfortable there in his tent.

Tomorrow, Noel could see that the route up the Rapadalen ought to be rather more straightforward. The map showed a continuous path, and he reasoned that this would be in reasonably good shape. The path that he had found on Nammásj should be fairly easy to follow down, and must lead to the main path. Ultimately, Noel was looking to get to a point where the main path went up the side of a mountain, Låddebákte, to the north of the valley. There he would leave the valley, to walk behind Låddebákte, and then drop down again to remeet the valley in its higher stages. But he wouldn't get that far tomorrow. There was another peak in the valley further up, Lulep Spádnek and perhaps he would try to camp on that, similarly to his campsite tonight.

Noel consumed his dinner. This time he just about managed to finish it, which was good. The day's exertion and fresh air seemed to have improved his appetite. He still didn't have room for a dessert though, although he had brought enough to have a dessert every day. So he finished off with a few squares of chocolate. He then got up, rinsed his spoon with some of the water from the couscous pouch, cleaned his teeth, and put the stove away. He took a bit of time to look around. There were a few gaps in the cloud and he could see some stars, so hopefully the weather tomorrow would be good, as predicted. It wasn't very late, only about 9pm, but Noel was happy just to lie down in his sleeping bag, and felt that he would probably go to sleep fairly readily. He was hoping to see the northern lights during his trip, although it looked as if the sky was too cloudy that evening, maybe another night.

It was always one of the pleasures of a hiking trip, for Noel, to review the day's photos while in his sleeping bag before going to sleep. So he got his camera out and scrolled through them. Some of the photos that he had taken in the evening over the delta looked fantastic and he was really pleased with them. He switched his camera off, and placed it to one side, to go to sleep.

Although Noel was experienced in the outdoors, camping on top of a mountain, even a small one like this, wasn't a typical thing for him to do. Better to camp somewhere sheltered, with water. It just seemed unintuitive to be camping up here. But Nammásj made such a good vantage point over the valley that Noel had decided to do it on this occasion, and he was glad of his decision. Noel's mind did start to wander to a group of Russian skiers he had once read about who in the 1950s camped near the top of a mountain in the Ural Mountains in the depths of winter. Their bodies had been found some weeks later, in the snow in various states of undress, scattered across the mountain below their tent. Conspiracy theorists had come up with explanations involving yetis and extra-terrestrials. But it was almost certain that the deaths of the skiers were due to extreme winds, and possibly an avalanche, forcing them out of their tent into bitterly cold temperatures which they could not possibly survive in overnight. And there was a similar incident that had happened here in Sweden, further to the south, where skiers had got caught out in a sudden storm with ferocious winds, and again not survived.

Noel was hardly in any danger of dying of exposure here in September. But he did worry about the possibility of the wind picking up in such an exposed location. If it did he might have to get up in the middle of the night and repitch his tent, which would not be much fun. He lay there for a bit and, after a while, started to doze off.

Suddenly there came a sound, "THUMP".

Something had just struck the outside of the tent. Noel froze in alarm. What on earth was that? Surely there was no-one else around on this mountain? He called out. "HELLO?" But there was no answer. An animal perhaps? He lay there for a bit, motionless, to see if he could hear anything else. But he heard nothing. He decided that it was no good, he was never going to get to sleep if he just lay there. So he got up, put his boots on and went out to investigate.

Noel shone his torch around. He was feeling nervous. The guy ropes of his tent were coated in reflective material to save people from tripping over them in the dark, and he found their reflections from his torch a bit disconcerting. He shone his torch all around, fearful of finding some eyeshine looking back at him. He called out again. But nothing. No reply, no movement. He went round to the other side of the tent, where he felt that the tent had been struck. A small, leafless branch was lying there. Had that been there earlier? Noel wasn't sure. He might well have not noticed it. Presumably it must have blown off a tree, although the nearest trees were not that close. That was what must have happened, concluded Noel. The wind was quite gusty after all. Strange though. Noel picked the branch up and, rather than throw it away, decided to put it inside the flysheet of his tent so that he would know it hadn't been a dream in the morning.

Noel went back to bed. For some time he just lay there, feeling on edge about what had just happened. But in time he was sound asleep.

## II

## Thursday 28th September

Noel had set his alarm for 6a.m., a little before sunrise. He was deeply asleep when it went off and he groaned to be disturbed so early. And it was cold in his tent. Getting up was not appealing. But he had decided to return to the summit of Nammásj to see the sunrise from there. It was such a special place. So he pulled himself out of his sleeping bag, put on several layers of clothing, put his boots on and got out of his tent. The branch that had disturbed him last night was still there, in the porch of his tent. Outside there was a frost.

Grabbing his camera and binoculars, Noel walked over to the vantage point where he had been the night before and looked across the delta. The sun started rising behind the lengthy expanses of pine forest that lay beyond Lájtávrre, stretching all the way back to Jokkmokk. The skies were clear, and it looked like being a beautiful crisp morning. It was exhilarating to see the sun lighting up the landscape, first the mountains, then reaching Noel himself, and then hitting the delta below. He stretched his arms up to maximise his exposure to the sun and soak up a little warmth from its rays. Slowly, the sun came up over the delta. With the golden autumn colour of the birch trees, and the blue of the sky reflected in the lakes and channels, it was stunning.

After 20 minutes or so, Noel turned around and walked back a bit to take in the view to the west. This was in the direction up Rapadalen, where his day's walk would lie. There was a fine view in that direction too, and better photo opportunities, given that the sun was now behind him. He had a clear view of a long extent of the Ráhpaädno River, winding its way down from the mountains. On the right two ridges ran down, one quite close, the other rather more distant. The distant one included Noel's intended campsite for the night, Lulep Spádnek. Beyond them, and south of the river, were the mountains of Gådoktjåhkkå and Bielloriehppe, each with quite a sprinkling of fresh snow from the day before. The terrain looked wild, and it invited exploration.

Noel walked back to his tent, had breakfast, packed up, took the tent down, and threw the branch from last night back at the trees. He decided that he had got too worked up about the branch hitting his tent. There was no-one else around, and clearly it had simply come off a tree.

Noel was on his way down the mountain by 8:30am. He was soon at the level of the Ráhpaädno and found himself joining the main trail along the valley. Downstream, he understood that this led to the point where the boat would normally pick up and drop off hikers. Up the valley was his direction for the day. Someone had clearly camped at this junction previously, as there were the remains of a camp fire.

Noel set off up the valley. He had not been too sure what to expect of the path here. Although it was marked on the map, it was not in any sense an official path, and was unlikely to be maintained. He had been concerned about getting caught up in trees and having to make his way through them like yesterday. But the path was good, and this possibility was looking unlikely. Occasionally it got a bit boggy, and there was ice on many of the puddles, but Noel was very thankful to find that boardwalks had been put in place across many of the boggier areas. Clearly some maintenance of the path was carried out. This walk looked as if it would go fairly smoothly, he concluded.

Noel continued walking. It was cold but so pleasant to be getting some sunshine and fresh air. His rucksack did not seem to have got any lighter and he kept retightening the waist and chest straps to take some of the weight off his shoulders. But at least the route was flat and easy to follow. He saw some very fresh animal scat on the trail, steaming a bit in the cold; clearly something else was using the trail. He sped up, to try to catch a glimpse of whatever it was, and there was more scat, but he never saw anything. There are a lot of wild animals in Sarek, including wolverine, lynx, bears, and wolves, and he would have been thrilled to see any of them. But they are incredibly shy, often nocturnal, and seem to have an ability to just merge into the forest at will. They have known man for too long and developed too much fear. The bears are not a concern like those of North America; they are too afraid of people to be of any real danger.  He kept his eyes peeled for anything that he might see. There were quite a few small birds flocking in the trees and at one point two capercaillies flew up on his approach, much like the grouse he had seen yesterday, only bigger. A vole, grey on the sides and rufous brown on its back, ran across the path before disappearing into a hole. What about lemmings, isn't this where they live, thought Noel. Perhaps it wasn't a lemming year. But mostly the forest was quite silent, and Noel saw little. But he just sensed that he was far from alone there.

Noel stopped for a break mid-morning. Nammásj was visible behind him, above the trees, having been lost behind them as he started walking on the main path. On either side of it were Skierffe and Tjahkelij, the three forming a stately group above the semi-bare birch trees.

Noel carried on. There were occasional stream crossings to be done, none of them very difficult. In July it might have been a different matter, with abundant meltwater from the winter's snow filling the streams. But right now, in September, it was easy. Indeed, one watercourse that he came upon was completely dry, just a channel of grey and white rocks, about five metres across, in the forest. He instinctively looked left and right before crossing it, as if the channel were a road, and there might have been traffic along it. It made him laugh.

As he was expecting, he saw no-one all morning. It started to feel relatively warm, in the sun at least. He made good progress and by midday was approaching the base of Lulep Spádnek, his planned campsite for the night. Its flanks were rather rocky with a lot of trees, and he began to question whether climbing another mountain to spend the night on was so appealing. He was doubtful that he would find a path here.

Noel continued. He arrived at a clearing, adjacent to the river, with a steep slope below it where the river had cut into the bank. He thought about stopping for lunch but it seemed a bit early. He carried on and soon came to a second, larger, clearing, again above a loose rocky slope leading down to the river. It would have been an excellent place to camp, he thought. He would be able to look out from his tent to see if any wildlife appeared on the opposite side of the river. But it was certainly too early in the day to set up camp. He decided instead to stop for lunch.

He spent about an hour having his lunch, enjoying his location. It was surprising how long could be spent, just having a simple lunch. But Noel wasn't in any special hurry. He was confident now that the route he had planned was not too ambitious. The path through Rapadalen was good. Beyond the valley, there was no path marked on the map, but that didn't matter as Noel would then be higher up, on tundra, above the treeline, and it should be easy to walk wherever he wanted.

At one point while he was sitting, a pair of red-breasted mergansers, a type of duck, appeared on the river, diving for invertebrates, letting the river carry them down as they looked for food, and Noel watched them for a while. The river was rocky, turbulent and blue, with fine sediment carried down from glaciers upstream. He was very admiring of how the ducks could appear so at ease looking for food in such a place.

Noel stood up, perhaps a little too quickly, as it left him feeling dizzy. Too much blood being allocated to digesting his food, and not enough being sent to his head. He stood still for a bit to let his blood rebalance, and then put his rucksack on. He decided that he wouldn't go up Lulep Spádnek. It looked too rocky and he was doubtful if he would find a good camping spot up there. He would carry on further up the valley.

He spent a while rounding the flank of Lulep Spádnek. The trail then deteriorated a bit. It was still there, but trees here were very thick, and had grown in on the path from either side so he often had to struggle to manoeuvre past their branches. At times he even resorted to walking backwards to push his rucksack through. There also quite a few small streams running over the ground, as if a bigger stream ahead had burst its banks.

Noel kept thinking that he could hear voices, and he stopped a couple of times to try to make them out more clearly. He cocked his ear to try to catch them better. The sound continued as he walked. He concluded that it must just have been the noise from the stream that he knew he was approaching. Perhaps in the same way that the mind often makes out faces in random shapes, so the mind often makes out voices, when there are none there.

After a short time, Noel reached the stream. It didn't look particularly deep, but it was broad. There was no way that he would be able to cross it safely by stepping from rock to rock. He was going to have to get his feet wet. So he sat down on the bank to take his boots and socks off and exchange them for sandals. As he was seated, a bluethroat, a thrush-like bird with a brilliant blue and red throat, hopped through the low levels of the streamside bushes to look at him, seemingly just out of curiosity, before hopping away again. It was nice to have the company, even if just for a short while.

Once he had his sandals on, Noel rolled his trouser legs up, got out and extended his trekking poles, tied his boots together by the laces, socks inside, put his rucksack back on, and hung the boots by the laces over his neck. He stepped out into the water, facing upstream.

Noel knew of course that the water would be cold, but he was still a bit taken aback by just how cold it was, almost as if it stung his feet. But at least his feet were getting a good wash. He pressed on, sideways across the stream. At most, the water only came up to his shins.

Bit by bit Noel sidestepped across the stream. Some of the underlying rocks were loose, but he always checked that each foot was steady before putting his weight on it. He was soon at the other side, his feet feeling fresh, but rather numb. He sat down, got his towel out from his rucksack, dried his feet off, put his socks and boots back on and repacked his rucksack, ready to continue.

What if Noel had slipped and fallen over while crossing the stream? Clearly he would have got wet and cold. But that was manageable. He kept his sleeping bag and spare clothes in a sealed dry bag in his rucksack. Wet clothes could dry out somewhat overnight. He would get over it in a few days. If he slipped and hit his head on a rock that was more of a worry. He could, in the most extreme case, knock himself out and drown. So, in order to keep his hands free for the case of a fall, he was sure always to keep them out of the loops on the handles of his trekking poles while crossing a river. Hopefully he would then be able to break his fall with his hands. If he slipped and broke his ankle or leg, then that was very serious, out here on his own.

For the case of serious accidents, Noel carried with him an emergency locator beacon, called a "ReachMe". This was a piece of electronics, of a size that he could fit in the palm of his hand,

and through which he could trigger an S.O.S. alert containing his location. This would be sent, via satellite, to the authorities back in the UK. They would then notify the Swedish Mountain Rescue Service, who would, Noel believed, send a helicopter. So breaking an ankle or leg out here should be survivable. If, in the most extreme case, Noel slipped, hit his head on a rock in the stream, and knocked himself out, then there was a chance that he could simply drown. He was aware of that, but it was far from likely, and it was a risk that he accepted. Mentally he was primed to do whatever was necessary to protect his head in the event of a fall in a river crossing.

Noel pressed on. With the time spent sitting down on either side of the stream, he had got a bit cold, and he needed to warm up. So he moved at a decent pace. He was not very aware of the Ráhpaädno now, and estimated that he must be six or seven hundred metres away from it. In time, he came across a low, wooded ridge, and decided to climb it, with a view to camping there for the night. There was a good location for his tent on top. He found a spot which was sheltered under the trees, but had a view out over a meadow below the ridge. There were the remains of a campfire, so clearly someone had camped there before. He pitched his tent. It was just after four o'clock.

It was too early for dinner, so he decided to take a walk around his elevated perch in the woods. Maybe he would see some wildlife. He put all his food in the watertight bag where his sleeping bag had been during the day and made sure to zip up both the inner and flysheet of the tent. The last thing he wanted was for an animal, such as a wolverine, to find his food while he was away from the tent. There is a reason why another name for the wolverine is "glutton". Returning to his tent and finding half of his food spoilt would be bad news indeed.

The ridge was bigger than Noel had appreciated, and there were other places on it where he could have camped. It felt secure to be up on the ridge, slightly above valley level, and he had a water source in the form of a stream running below, along one side of the base of the ridge.

After walking around for a bit, Noel returned to his tent, disappointed in his search for wildlife. It was still quite early for dinner, but more pleasant to eat while it was still light, so Noel rummaged around in his dry bag for a ready meal, landed himself a chicken curry, and got ready preparing it. He found himself a spot for his dinner, looking out over the open ground below, and consumed it, contentedly.

Noel finished his dinner and cleaned up. It was now starting to get dark, and he felt ready for bed. It was also getting cold, quite rapidly, due to the still clear skies. It was quite early, but he was tired. He was starting to live according to the rhythm of the sun, getting up and going to bed early, instead of living partly by electric light, and it felt good. He retreated into his tent and, as in the previous evenings, he got his map out and examined it by torchlight to plan his route for the next day.

Noel had now come about two thirds of the way along the Rapadalen from Aktse to the point where the path would leave the Rapadalen, to climb up and pass behind Låddebákte, before re-entering the higher stretches of the valley close to the treeline. He considered the possibility of continuing to walk up the Rapadalen valley and skirting around Låddebákte on its southwest side, but, while the climb would be less, the distance would be more and he would be faced with a lot more trees to bash through, where, according to the map, there was no path. Near Skårkistugan, the place where the path turned off out of the valley, was what looked like another delta, smaller than that immediately above Aktse, but with a lot of lakes and channels. At the point where the path out of the valley reached the valley edge there was a small lake. It looked like potentially a very good campsite. The view from there over the Skårkistugan delta ought to be magnificent. It was quite high up, around 1,000m, so he counted on a cold night, but he was equipped for that. In fact, why not two nights, he asked himself. He could leave his tent, climb up Låddebákte, and then return to his tent for a second night. The views ought to be spectacular.

Noel got up and out of the tent to clean his teeth before going to sleep. The night was starlit, cold, and very quiet. He returned to his tent, got into his sleeping bag, and reflected on the day. He was pleased with how the trip was going. It had been important to pick something that challenged him, and being out here alone in the wilderness did that. But at the same time it was important not to be challenged too much, or the trip would be an endurance rather than an adventurous holiday. He felt that he had got the balance about right. Noel turned off his headtorch and turned over to go to sleep. He lay there for a while, on the edge of sleepfulness.

Noel heard a slight sound which startled him.  He sat up and turned his head to try to catch it. He held his breath for a moment so that there would be no sound from his breathing. There definitely was a sound that he could hear. It was very quiet, but it was as if someone was playing a badly tuned radio. For the second night in a row, Noel was getting the impression that there was someone else in the forest. He decided that if there was, he wanted to go and find them. He couldn't just lie there wondering.

Noel put some clothes on, and stuck his head out of the tent. Immediately he was dumbstruck. Taking place outside was the most magnificent display of the Northern Lights imaginable. He stood up and admired them for a moment. Great arcs of light shimmering across the sky in front of the stars. He found it frightening, in a way, being all alone in the wilderness with this amazing otherworldly display of light. He stood very still and he could still hear the out-of-tune radio. It did seem as if the sound might be coming from the Northern Lights. It seemed strange. Noel knew that the Northern Lights were produced well up in the earth's atmosphere, maybe 50-200 miles up. So how could they be producing a sound at ground level? He didn't know. But clearly it was more likely that the sound was coming from the Lights than that someone nearby was trying to tune their radio in.

Noel was correct in his understanding that the Northern Lights are produced high in the earth's atmosphere. But he was unaware that they can, under certain conditions, be associated with sounds at ground level, much as he had heard, although sometimes including claps as well. The process is not well understood but it seems that these sounds occur when air, warmed during the day by the sun at ground level, rises during a very still night, and forms an inversion layer, around 70 metres above the ground. Negative ions get trapped below this layer of warm air, and positive ions get trapped above it. The inversion layer is electrically insulating, but the electrical potential across it can be broken down by the same solar radiation that causes the Northern Lights. When this strikes the insulating layer it causes an electrical current to flow across the insulating layer. When this flows weakly it creates the sounds like a radio. When there is a complete breakdown of the electrical potential it causes a sudden discharge and a clap, similar in concept to a lightning strike, although of much less force. That was what he was hearing.

Noel wanted to get a better view. It had indeed become very cold. So he grabbed his down jacket and a woollen hat, as well as his camera and headtorch, and walked down to the meadow below, to be out of the trees. The Lights were stunning. Partly obscured by Skårki, the mountain to his north, they nonetheless extended well beyond this to cover a substantial portion of the sky. He watched, feeling appreciative of all the efforts that he had gone to to witness this spectacular sight. He sat down in the cold grass to be more steady and take some photos. He experimented with different settings on his camera as he knew it wasn't going to be easy. But he was wary of using his camera too much in the cold, as he only had one spare battery and knew how much the camera's battery would drain in the cold. After about fifteen minutes the lights became weaker, and quite quickly they stopped altogether. He stood up, and waited a further ten minutes before deciding that that was probably it for now, that he was getting too cold, and he would go back up to his tent.

He walked quite briskly up the slope to his tent, his breath showing up in the light of his headtorch as it condensed in the cold air. Although he had got really cold it had clearly been worthwhile for such great views of the Lights. This trip was turning out to be a big success. Fantastic views that morning from Nammásj, and now the Northern Lights. It had been a great day. He got back to his tent.

What he saw at his tent made him gasp. He had zipped his tent up. He was sure that he had zipped his tent up. But his tent was open, the fly sheet neatly buttoned back to the side. And in the entrance to the tent someone had placed three angular grey rocks neatly in a line. He had been sure that there was no-one around. He had walked all around the ridge before dinner and seen no-one. Yet evidently somebody was trying to disturb him, and it wasn't funny. Were they still around? He looked around, behind all the trees, behind the tent, feeling intense discomfort about what had happened. There was no sign of anyone. Who would do such a thing? Could there perhaps be someone in the tent? He picked up one of his trekking poles and used it to check either side of the tent door and under the sleeping bag. There was no-one inside. Quickly he checked that his wallet and passport were still in place, fearful of an approach from someone outside while he did so. They were both there. He put them in his pockets and stood outside the tent for a while, trying to regain his composure.

Someone was trying to frighten Noel. Maybe it had been done as a joke. But what to do? He couldn't just let it pass. So he decided that he would at least try to find whoever had done this. They must be camping nearby. He took a photo of his tent, with the stones, as evidence, reclosed the zips, threw the stones off the ridge down into the meadow, and set off to walk around the ridge. He had seen before that there were other camping sites there.

Noel walked right around the ridge where he had walked earlier before dinner, feeling a mixture of anger towards whoever had done this, and some fear. Any tent in the area should show up well as there would probably be some reflective material on it. He shone his torch down into the meadow as he walked around the ridge to see if the malefactor's tent might be there. He covered every part of the ridge. He called out for a response, but none came. After 40 minutes he had found nothing, absolutely nothing, and he was feeling really cold. There was no sign of anyone at all having been there. He was back at his tent. Fortunately no-one had interfered with it this time.

It occurred to Noel, with some alarm, that the perpetrator might now be inside his tent. He hit it with his trekking pole and shouted "Oy", but there was no response. Gingerly he opened it up and checked inside as before. It was unoccupied and seemed to be untouched. He stood outside, wondering what to do now.

It was no good. Noel couldn't go back to sleep in that tent. Someone was trying to scare him. Perhaps it was just a joke. But the way the perpetrator had carried out the act and just disappeared, meant that any humour was lost. If Noel tried to sleep, he would be anxious all night that that person was going to come back to disturb him further. Had the person who did this also thrown the branch at him the previous night? Possibly. If so, that would make it even more disturbing, because it meant that someone was following him. Otherwise how could they have found his campsite this evening? It was a horrible situation and he felt very shaken.

Noel decided that the best thing to do would be to try to shake whoever this was off his trail. He had less than a day's walking to go before he would be out of the trees. Then he would be on the tundra. Anyone thinking of disturbing him once he was up there would be much more visible. What he would do now would be to take down his tent, walk further up the trail, and find somewhere off the path and hidden to camp. He would sleep prepared to defend himself, should he need to do so.

So Noel began to dismantle his tent. He was not happy about the situation at all. It was extremely cold, and he would have liked to have been going to sleep. He packed up his rucksack and tent and walked down the slope of the ridge, in the direction of the continuation of his hike up the valley. When he got to the meadow he switched off his torch. He wanted to do everything he could to avoid being followed. There was no moon, nor any further sign of the Northern Lights, but the stars were bright. He looked behind himself repeatedly as he walked across the meadow to check that he wasn't being followed. He saw no-one.

Once he got into the trees on the far side of the meadow, Noel found that it was too dark to walk without his headtorch. His torch had a facility to be switched to red light, so he used this, in order to have enough light to walk by, and at the same time be less visible to anyone following him. He kept looking behind himself, but saw nothing. At one point something ran off into the forest, startling him. Maybe just another roe deer, he figured. It certainly didn't sound human. After about 600 metres, he decided to head off and look for a campsite. He felt that he now had enough distance from his original site to hopefully not be found by whoever was seeking to disturb him. He cursed as he kept tripping over fallen branches as he walked. At what felt like a good 200 metres into the forest, he found a suitable spot to camp and stopped. He looked all around. Still there was no sign of anything or anyone else around. So he put his tent up, got into his sleeping bag, and looked forward to morning. His trekking poles, shortened to be of potential use for self-defence, lay beside him. It was almost 11p.m.

## III

## Friday 29<sup>th</sup> September

Noel's alarm woke him at 6a.m as it had done the day before. It was very cold in the tent and he soon started thinking of the event of the night before. What was supposed to be a nice experience in Sarek was now looking a bit stressful. Also, he hadn't really had enough sleep, and it was going to be painful to face the cold and get out of his sleeping bag. But, driven by his desire to move on further from the ridge, and to avoid any chance of being found in his tent by whomever had disturbed him, he got up, dressed, and out of the tent.

Outside it was cloudy, with a heavy frost. Noel stamped his feet a bit to warm up, and looked around to check that no-one had approached the tent overnight, or was now near it. There was no sign. He got his stove out, lit it, and put some water on the boil. He stamped his feet and blew into his hands to warm himself up. The spot where he had pitched his tent was not a very comfortable one, awkwardly positioned between branches of adjacent trees and fallen branches on the ground. Noel hadn't been feeling fussy about such things in thick of the night.

Once the water had boiled, Noel prepared himself a coffee and selected a dehydrated breakfast to eat. It meant a lot to be having hot food and coffee on a cold morning like this. He got back inside his tent to consume his breakfast and consider again his route for the day.

There remained about five miles to walk up the valley before the route would take Noel up out of it to pass alongside Låddebákte. The valley was relatively narrow along this stretch, with the mountain, Skårki, rising steeply above it to the north. Noel considered taking a route through the trees instead of the path, so as to avoid whomever seemed to be following him. But the narrowness of the valley here meant that it really wasn't practical to do anything other than take the path. If he met anyone on the path he would certainly raise the issue of what had happened the previous night with them.

By 7:30 Noel was ready to depart. He wasn't so hopeful about it warming up today, given that it was cloudy. So he wrapped up well. He had some salopettes designed for walking, so put those on, and he also wore a fleece and woollen hat.

Noel set off. Whilst he hadn't been so preoccupied by it while he was getting ready, once he was walking the previous night's occurrence started coming back to him. As he went, he kept looking back behind himself to see if anyone was there. He saw no-one. In a way, he would rather find someone to talk to about it, whether they were the perpetrator or not. But there was no sign of anyone else on the trail. The valley was as beautiful as ever, and again it seemed to be quite channelled between its bounding mountains, Skårki to the north and Bielloriehppe to the south. And, as lower down there had been a delta between the mountains, here again the river was broken up, forming a number of channels and small lakes in the flat valley floor.

At one point, Noel came to an open, grassy area, similar to that where he had viewed the Northern Lights the previous evening. The far side of it was quite untidy, with some large fallen trees and a big rock. Or was it a rock? He got his binoculars out and had a closer look. It was a moose! A huge moose just standing there, half in and half out of the undergrowth. That was great. He had really wanted to see a moose. So, for a better view, he decided to skirt around the meadow a bit, off the path. As he got closer, suddenly the ground shook as he realised that there were in fact four moose there and they were all taking fright at him and stampeding off. It was curious to see such huge animals in the forest, and surprising how well they had been able to hide up until then.

Noel was sorry that he had frightened the moose. It had seemed improbable in a way that such a huge animal would be afraid of him. But moose are widely hunted in Sweden, if not in the Sarek National Park, and so their fear is only natural. Strangely, the moose all stopped after thundering along for about ten yards. They stood, again half obscured by the low vegetation, but easily visible to Noel now that he knew they were there. Surely they were no safer from him than before? Did they think that they were now invisible? It was as if they had got frightened, run a bit, and decided that that was enough activity for now. Maybe moose are not the brightest animals, thought Noel. He observed the moose for a bit, and the moose observed him. After a while he decided that it was time to move on.

As he continued, Noel started to pass between small lakes and river channels. Snow was falling in light flurries. It was all rather peaceful, with the sense of the river flowing somewhere to his left, and the steep slopes of Skårki up to his right. At one point he heard a bugling sound, which he recognised immediately – cranes. He heard them trumpeting for a while, and then they were up, a pair of them circling around over the river, visible from in between the trees. They were a beautiful, graceful sight, flying against the cold grey mountain on the other side of the valley. No doubt they would soon be heading off, down to spend the winter in France or Spain.

There were also reindeer in the valley. Noel didn't see any in the forest, but he occasionally saw them sitting and standing around on sand banks by the river. He had imagined that they would be busy fattening themselves up for winter, but mostly they seemed just to be sitting around, with not much to do. Soon the Sámi herdsmen would be rounding them up for selective slaughter, before travelling down with them to the forests to the east to spend the winter.

Presently Noel arrived at Skårkistugan, where the path turned up to the right to leave the valley. Noel was aware that there was a mountain hut here, and the path carried on straight ahead, presumably to that hut. He could perhaps have spent the night there. But after the events of the previous night he preferred to try not to be found again, and the hut would be an obvious place to look for him. In any case he didn't know if the hut would be open. So, after a short break to consume a cereal bar, and remove a couple of layers of clothing for the more arduous ascent that he would now be making, he took the path to the right, up the side of the valley.

Within about 40 minutes, Noel found himself starting to come out of the trees. The treeline here in the Arctic is only at 700 metres above sea level, and Noel was reaching that height. Further up, a steep drop down into a gulley was necessary to cross a stream. It was striking how this gulley was full of trees; clearly the shelter from being close to the water and out of the wind made the difference between the environment being viable for a tree and not viable. Noel also appreciated the shelter of the gulley, and decided to take his lunch here.

After lunch, Noel climbed up out of the gulley and continued on the path up to a small pass. Beyond here was a high lake which drained out to the Ráhpaädno on the other side of Låddebákte, some distance above where Noel had left the river. He decided to stop for a moment at the pass and take in the view. This was extensive back down the Rapadalen. He could see where he had camped the previous night (both locations!), with Tjahkelij in the background. Nammásj and Skierffe were hidden behind ridges in the valley. Closer in, and below him, Noel could see the delta that he had walked past that day, with its many lakes and river channels. In the other direction, up the river, lay quite a large flat area where another river, the Sarvesvágge, joined the Ráhpaädno. This area is known as "Rovdjurstorget", meaning "predator square", as footprints of lynx, bear, wolf and wolverine have all been found there. It would have been an interesting location for Noel to spend some time. Maybe on the next visit, he thought, noting also that it was hard to make out anything square in the terrain there, the area was more of a triangle really.

Although it was early, Noel decided that he would look for somewhere to camp in the area overnight. A spot where he could look out over Rapadalen would be wonderful. The alternative was to continue past the high lake and then skirt along the side of a mountain north of there, called "Bielatjåhkkå". Camping close to the lake looked a bit bleak and if he camped in the area where he was, he would be able to keep an eye out for anyone who might follow him up from the main valley. The main path was close to a stream, so Noel filled his cooking pot and water bottle from that as he had done before spending the night on Nammásj. He then left the path and followed the stream round up to a small lake, with occasional reindeer jogging away from him as he went, and doubled back to a position in a hollow, about 60 metres across, looking out across Rapadalen. There was a rocky bluff on one side, but the location was grassy and out of the wind and just what that Noel wanted. He immediately set to work in erecting his tent, oriented so as to have a view over the valley from the porch. Below his tent was a stretch of grass leading down to quite a steep cliff above Rapadalen.

Once his tent was in place, Noel put his salopettes and down jacket on, and sat down to appreciate the view. It was a great overlook that he had, and he was happy to spend the best part of an hour taking it in. Immediately opposite him, across the Rapadalen was the large pyramid-shaped peak of Bielloriehppe, its slopes falling sharply down to the valley. At its foot were two triangular-shaped lakes, and the main course of the Ráhpaädno. Bielloriehppe clearly reflected in the lakes. Also visible was the hut that he had bypassed at Skårkistugan, secluded deeply in the forest, with its chimney and red roof and walls. At one point, he spotted through his binoculars another moose. It was standing by the river, occasionally venturing into it slightly. It looked as if it wanted to cross. But it sat down, clearly not comfortable about making the crossing.

Noel's thoughts turned to events back home, and what had led him to venture on his own to this remote location. Apart from the disturbance of the previous night, he was growing comfortable in his isolation, and felt some apprehension about his return to society in a week's time. How would it be just to stay here until forced out by the winter snows? If he could have brought more food it would have been rather an appealing idea, just him and nature, going on small walks. But he couldn't have carried much more weight than he had done. Or maybe a hearty Swedish girl would hike by, invite him back to her mountain cabin, and they could get lost to the world forever, up here in Lapland, living off reindeer and wild berries. The chance would be a fine thing.

From this point on in his hike, until shortly before the end at Suorva, Noel was going to be above the trees. This meant that he had an opportunity, albeit modest, to supplement his diet. He was able to pick bilberries, similar to blueberries. Although perhaps a little past their prime in September, and eaten in vast amounts by both bears and reindeer, there were still lots of them where he had camped. He got up, got out his drinking cup and filled it to the brim with berries, ready to supplement his dessert and tomorrow's breakfast, eating quite a few as he went.

Berries picked, Noel turned his thoughts to dinner. Chicken Chow Mein followed by apple crumble with added bilberries tonight. It all looked good, and he was hungry. Bilberries were in fact a small part of the calculation that Noel had made for his calory intake for the trip in order to ensure that he had enough food when setting off.

Noel cooked and ate his dinner outside. It was cold, but he was well wrapped up and the view as the sun set beyond Rapadalen was wonderful. Also, he was quite keen to keep an eye out for anyone else who might be making their way up towards him; he didn't want a repeat of last night. He had thought that it might snow quite heavily that day, but for the most part it had held off. But as he finished his dinner, it did start snowing, and more heavily than it had done during the day. Eventually it drove him inside his tent.

Noel got ready for bed, into his sleeping bag, and as on previous nights, looked over his map to plan the next day. He decided that, as long as there wasn't too much snow overnight, he would climb Låddebákte, and return to his tent to spend a second night in this location. He could take a lunch with him. It would be about a 500-metre climb, perhaps a bit of scramble, and at the summit he should have a great view across to Rovdjurstorget. Maybe a lynx would be strolling along by the river for him to view from up on high. He had a look over the day's photos on his camera. He then set his alarm on his phone for 7a.m. (climbing Låddebákte should only take up half the day, so there was no need for such an early start as before), and then turned over to go to sleep.

# IV

## Saturday 30<sup>th</sup> September

Noel awoke to the sound of a sudden snort outside his tent. Then footsteps. He was startled. He was starting to get a bit on edge about the various disturbances outside his tent. But it was light. At least nothing had disturbed him in the dark this time. Some more footsteps. Reindeer, thought Noel to himself. He clapped his hands and shouted out, "GO ORRN." The reindeer, if that's what it was, ran off a bit. Noel sat up and put his head out of his tent. There were three reindeer, staring at him from about 20 metres away. He was happy to have their company. He saw that it had snowed in the night, a depth of maybe about half an inch, and that there were reindeer footprints all around. The reindeer stared at him for a bit before cantering off, but staying within view. There are no wild reindeer in this part of Scandinavia – these ones would all belong to Sámi herders.

Noel rubbed his eyes, and put on some clothes and his boots. He climbed out of his tent and looked around the area where he had camped. Plenty of reindeer footprints in the snow. No sign of any human footprints, thankfully. That was good. It looked as if the crazy man from the valley had stayed down where he belonged.

There was quite a bit of snow higher on the mountains, and it had settled some way down where Noel was camped, almost down to the valley bottom. The tops of Skårki and Bielloriehppe were enveloped in swirling cloud. Hopefully that cloud would lift, he thought, and give wonderful views from Låddebákte. It looked promising for the planned climb, although the fresh snow was a concern; the risk of slipping on it was significant. He went back into his tent to sort out some breakfast.

Noel sat outside to eat his breakfast. It was chilly and crisp, but the view was so wonderful that he didn't mind feeling a bit cold.

When he had eaten about half of his breakfast, the sun started poking out through the clouds, from the direction of Aktse. Noel realised that he needed his sunglasses, so went back into his tent to fetch them. He had been reluctant to bring sunglasses when he packed – why would he need them in Lapland in September? But of course the possibility of snow meant that they were very much needed and he was thankful that he had them with him. In fact, if the sun came right out, he would probably need to put on some sunscreen at some point. Maybe he could even get a tan.

The snow was starting to melt, and Noel decided that his climb up Låddebákte was on. He would need to take care with regard to any ice, and if it got too slippery, he would have to turn back. But the snow wasn't deep, and he was hopeful that it would continue to melt as the day went on. He emptied out his rucksack inside his tent, and packed his sleeping bag (in case of emergencies), some food and water, spare clothing, his torch, and his camera and binoculars and map. He propped his rucksack up against a rock, zipped up the tent, marked the location of his tent on his gps unit, said goodbye to the reindeer, and by 9a.m. he was off, looking for his way up the mountain.

Noel began by going down to the small lake which he had passed on his way up on the previous day. There was too much of a cliff above him to ascend the mountain directly from his campsite. So he skirted the lake, with the mountain to his left. There was no very obvious route up the mountain. There were no streams coming down it which he could follow, and it was a very hummocky shape mountain, with lots of loose rocks. It seemed unlikely that there would be any path up it as It was too rocky, and presumably not much frequented. He continued along the base of the mountain for a while and gradually the slope of Låddebákte began to look less forbidding. So he turned left, and began to go directly up it. It was hard work, quite steep and with a lot of loose rocks, and some snow. He needed to use his hands

43

for balance at times. Before long, he was too hot, and he stopped to take some layers off. A snow bunting, a small bird, brown and white at this time of year, which feeds off seeds and insects blown onto patches of snow, flew in, and then off again. It was the first he had seen on the trip, and it gave him more of a feeling of being in the mountains now. Also, as he climbed higher, some of the highest peaks of Sarek started to come into view. To the north he could see Sarektjåhkkå, the highest mountain in the park, and second highest mountain in Sweden. Below it lay the upper reaches of the Rapadalen, where he planned to walk the next day. Further to the right another large mountain, Ähpár, started to come into view, behind the large boulder-strewn mass of Bielatjåhkkå. Noel continued scrambling up, kicking snow off the rocks as he went. Because of the nature of the ground, his progress wasn't very fast, but he kept going and within a couple of hours the mountain started to level out. He had reached the summit ridge and had a marvellous view down to the Rapadalen. He doubled back on himself to follow the ridge around to the summit, and soon stood there. Previous climbers had constructed a small cairn there and he was happy to see it. It was good to feel that he had some connection with other hikers over the years. He put on some extra layers of clothing, and had a good look around. The sun had now come out fully, and he felt very contented, his issues back home a long way away.

The view from the mountaintop was, as always in Rapadalen, spectacular. Noel could see the various lakes and river channels of the higher delta, and beyond them, the tops of Nammásj and Skierffe were now showing again. He could see nearly all of the route that he had taken yesterday. To the north was a fine array of mountains – Sarektjåhkkå, Ähpár and Skårki. These were the highest mountains of the Sarek National Park. He had read that the rocks that they are made up of are 400 million years old and were formed in a period of mountain building related to the closure of the great Iapetus Ocean which lay between the continents of Laurentia (now much of North America and Greenland) and Baltica (now Scandinavia and western Russia). Once, the mountains had probably been as high as the Himalayas. Then they were eroded, then uplifted again, and most recently eroded by glaciation to take their present form. They had certainly had quite a life. Noel would dearly like to climb some of the largest ones someday. But now was not a good time of year as there would be a lot of snow on each of them. In addition, Sarektjåhkkå required the crossing of a glacier for which, if ever he did it, he would need company, plus a rope and crampons to navigate the glacier. In relation to Ähpár, the mountain on the horizon to the northeast, Noel had read that according to Sámi legend, this mountain is the haunt of demons, and contains the ghost of an illegitimate child. The mountain was indeed rather angular and forbidding. He reflected that Sarek was a very spiritual place and that it was no wonder that there were stories like that about it. Rapadalen was so beautiful that it was almost supernaturally so. He was due to walk past Ähpár in the coming days. He would be on extra good behaviour and hopefully the spirits wouldn't trouble him. But, as long as the ghost of the illegitimate child was going to stay inside the mountain, and not trouble Noel, that was fine by him.

Then Noel had an awful realisation. In addition to reading about the spirits of Ähpár, he remembered that he had also read about how there were Sámi sacrificial sites in Sarek. One was located at the base of Skierffe. Were those reindeer antlers that he had thrown into the lake two days ago something to do with the sacrificial site? It did perhaps look as if the bones had been lain there by someone rather than just being where a reindeer had died. He felt a bit guilty. Perhaps he shouldn't have done that. Oh well, no-one was going to know about it anyway, but perhaps he had better be on extra good behaviour from now on.

Noel got out his lunch and scanned Rovdjurstorget, of which he had a good view, with his binoculars. It was a bit far below him to offer much chance of seeing wildlife, realistically, and he didn't have any luck.

Lunch over, Noel decided to walk around the crest of the mountain to the west and then head north for better views of the higher stretches of Rapadalen, and his planned route for tomorrow. It wasn't very easy, as he had to take a lot of care with the loose rocks and snow, and there was a big cliff to his left, but he was happy to go slowly as he had plenty of time. The walk was very airy, with wonderful views. But it was exhilarating

Eventually the ridge started dropping to the northeast, down to the pass behind Låddebákte. There is a sizeable lake in this pass, with an outlet down to the northwest, to the higher part of the Rapadalen. Noel had finished his water while up on the mountain. He had topped it up with snow, but this wasn't melting very well. So he was pleased to find a stream when he got down to the pass. He refilled his water bottle and drank a few mouthfuls. The path which he had taken up the Rapadalen ran along the north side of the lake. He could have crossed the stream to follow that back to his campsite. But, to avoid repeating the route he would be doing the next day, he opted instead to stay south of the lake and make his way back across the rocky tundra. The snow had now all melted at this level. The lake was rather bleak, and devoid of life being almost 1,000 metres above sea level. Noel did see a flock of eight ducks, long-tailed ducks, sitting on it. It seemed strange to him that they would stay up here, so late in the season. They didn't seem to be doing much, just bobbing about. Why didn't they fly somewhere warmer? He walked on, back towards his tent.

Noel approached the small ridge behind his tent, and couldn't help feeling some apprehension. He had taken all of his valuables with him, but at the back of his mind was still the fear that someone might have interfered with it, as had happened the other night. What if the tent wasn't there at all? That would be a shock.

Noel passed the small lake behind his tent, and climbed up to the ridge. His tent was still in place, and untouched. The reindeer that had disturbed him in the morning looked to have moved on. It was 4p.m. He unpacked his rucksack, put on his warmest clothes, and spent some time looking down the valley. Nothing was moving in it. The sky was starting to show some high, wispy, cirrostratus clouds, however. He was aware that this can signal the approach of a warm front, and precipitation. It looked as if the weather was going to deteriorate overnight.

Noel cooked his dinner, and ate it in the tent. It would have been rewarding to have had it outside while admiring the view, but it was getting a little too cold. He had now got through about a third of his food, and tomorrow his rucksack ought to be appreciably lighter. He felt very well. He only had mild discomfort in his feet from all the walking, and a bit of neckache from his rucksack, but otherwise felt strong, and quite able to continue. Tomorrow he would walk back past the high lake, down to rejoin the Rapadalen but staying above the river, and then along to the northeast, past the base of Ähpár with its child and demons. It should be a fairly straightforward day, with no ascent.

After finishing his dinner, Noel went outside to brush his teeth and put the stove away. The cirrostratus clouds had built a bit more. He estimated that it would probably start raining or snowing in the early hours. He returned to his tent and tightened up the guy ropes, checking that the fly sheet was not in contact with the inner at any point, so that he would remain dry overnight.

Noel got into his tent and into his sleeping bag. He looked over the photos that he had taken that day; he was very pleased with them. This was such a wonderful campsite, he thought. Stunning scenery, no-one around for miles. It felt very healthy just being here with all this fresh air, eating bilberries and going on a day hike. He was looking forward to continuing on to the north where the scenery would be quite different, more tundra-like. He rolled himself over in his sleeping bag and was soon asleep.

## V

## Night of Saturday 30[h] September

Noel guessed that perhaps he had been sleeping for an hour or so, but he found himself wide awake. There was some light coming into the tent, and he could tell that the moon must have risen. He didn't know why he was awake, but he didn't have the feeling that he was quickly going to get back to sleep. He rolled over onto his back and looked up.

And froze in horror. There was the shadow of a man looming over his tent, right above his head. It was unmistakeable. Someone was standing right outside. The man wasn't moving but Noel could see the person's chest expanding and contracting slightly as he breathed. Noel closed his eyes. "This is a dream" he told himself. He heard the figure clearing its throat. It was undoubtedly a person standing there. Noel opened his eyes again. The figure was still there. He bit his finger. It hurt. He definitely was not dreaming. Somebody was standing right against his tent, not moving. It was definitely not a reindeer.

What to do? Why would somebody stand right by his tent like that, without making a sound? He was terrified. He lay there, as if paralysed, hoping that the person would just go away and he could pretend to himself that this hadn't happened. But the person just stood there.

Noel couldn't lie there all night, staring at this figure. He could call out. But he was afraid of what the person might then do. The behaviour of the man in just standing there, not doing anything, was very aggressive. Noel would be defenceless in his sleeping bag. He decided that he would prefer to confront the man standing up, rather than remonstrating with him from in his sleeping bag. He was going to need to get up and out of his tent.

Putting his hand on the zip of his sleeping bag, Noel counted down in his head. "Three...two...one" and he unzipped his sleeping bag. It jammed. He pulled it up again. He noticed the person moving. He pulled the zip down again. This time it went. He grabbed his headtorch, unzipped the inner compartment of the tent and then the fly sheet. He jumped out, barefoot, put his torch on his head and turned it on. Something was running, away up the hill. Noel shouted out, after it "HEY". The figure kept running away. Noel ran after it. Then the figure got to a rock, stood up on it and turned to face him.

Noel froze in total disbelief. Out here, in the middle of nowhere, in the middle of the night, stood something so out of place as to be terrifying. There was a child standing in front of him. A boy of maybe fourteen years of age, barefoot and seemingly wearing only reindeer skin. In his hands were two reindeer antlers. His hair was unkempt and his face muddied. The boy just stood and grinned at Noel. He just couldn't believe it. Was he really seeing this?

Was this boy a Sámi? Perhaps. Noel wasn't familiar with the Sámi people, but he didn't imagine for a moment that they still dressed in reindeer skins, let alone allowed their children to run around unaccompanied deep in the mountains on a cold night.

"WHO ARE YOU? WHERE ARE YOUR PARENTS?" Noel shouted. The boy just laughed.

Noel remembered the story of the illegitimate child of Ähpár, and felt a deep chill coming over him. Surely not. Surely this can't be anything to do with that, he told himself. Was he going mad?

The boy turned, and ran again, this time to stand on a rock. Noel stared as he threw each of the reindeer antlers out into the distance. Noel was reminded of what he had done back in the

50

boulder field below Skierffe. Did the boy somehow know about that? Surely that wasn't possible.

Noel ran after the boy. "Please leave me alone!" he shouted. The boy ran off down the slope, towards the small lake, laughing. But Noel couldn't keep running after the boy, it was too cold and he had no shoes on. And anyway, what was the point? What would he do if the caught up with him?

Dejectedly, Noel returned to his tent. What to do now? Something else beyond the presence of the boy concerned him. Had he really been tall enough to cast the shadow that he had seen over his tent? He had been under the impression that it was an adult man standing by his tent. The boy's shadow might have been lengthened if he had been standing a bit distant from the tent but the shadow seemed to have an adult's build. And Noel had felt that he could hear the person breathing, so he must have been close to the tent. What on earth was going on? He was cold so he decided to get into his tent and take stock of the situation.

Noel sat in his tent, not daring to get into his sleeping bag, and clasping his knees, thinking over what had just happened. He felt vulnerable – presumably this person or persons might come back at any time. But what to do? He decided that firstly he would like to have something to hand to defend himself with, so he got out of his tent to collect his trekking poles which were on the opposite side from the entrance. He looked around with his torch as he got out to see if he could see someone, but he saw no-one. He brought the trekking poles into the tent and shortened them down so as to be usable as a weapon if so needed.

Noel decided that he had four options. Firstly, he could repitch his tent as he had done previously. But, if the perpetrator had found him where he was this evening, away from the path, wouldn't they be just as likely to find him again if he camped somewhere else? There were no trees that he could hide his tent amongst up here. Secondly, he could get dressed properly, and go out to look for whoever was doing this. But such a search could take all night, and he would have to leave his tent, during which time someone might interfere with it. Thirdly, he could get dressed and just sit outside his tent, keeping watch. But that wasn't very appealing, he would just get too cold. Or fourthly he could try to go back to sleep, and hope that nothing further would happen.

Eventually, Noel decided that what he would do would be to get dressed, put his boots on, and attempt to sleep in his tent, like that. He could unzip his sleeping bag entirely and use it like a blanket. He would keep the flysheet of his tent unzipped, but pegged down, and the inner entirely unzipped. If somebody came again, he would jump out and confront them immediately. If he made it through the night without any more disturbances, he would decide what to do in the morning. Whether he would feel like hiking further into the park with the prospect of this sort of thing happening again, he would have to see tomorrow.

After putting on most of his clothes, Noel lay in his tent, going over in his head what had happened. He doubted whether he would sleep at all, he was so on edge. He wished it could be morning.

Half an hour later, Noel was half asleep.

"THWAK". Something hit Noel's tent poles with a force. Bleary-eyed, Noel jumped up and out of the tent. The same boy as before was running away up the slope, a reindeer's antler again in his hand, seemingly the implement that he had used to strike the tent. Noel ran after him, shouting at him to stop. Within about thirty yards, Noel caught the child, by his reindeer skin. "WHAT THE HELL ARE YOU DOING?" he shouted. The boy attempted to wriggle free. Noel caught the boy by his wrist.

Immediately that Noel did so, a roar came out from the bluff above the campsite. In horror, He looked up, and saw that there was a cloaked figure standing on the top, his face darkened. He recoiled in pain as the child bit him on the arm, and then ran off into the darkness. The figure on the bluff didn't look at Noel but stared fixedly at one of the distant mountains. Its whole body seemed to be quivering. The figure pushed forward with its feet and sent a torrent or rocks down towards where Noel was standing.

Slowly the figure opened its mouth and inhaled deeply. "GO" it bellowed without either taking its eyes off the horizon or ceasing to quiver.

"What do you want?" cried Noel, struggling to hide his distress, "Am I doing something wrong? All I'm doing is camping here."

"TAKE YOUR TENT AND GO," repeated the figure. It then picked up a rock and threw it at Noel's tent.

It was clearly no use arguing with this figure. Noel held his hands up in front of him in surrender. He would have to leave. This spot which had seemed such an idyllic campsite had turned into a nightmare of one.

"It's OK, I'm going. I'm going," he cried, in terror, and almost in tears. "I don't know what your problem is, just leave me alone."

Noel ran back to his tent. He couldn't bear to take his eyes off the figure on the bluff, who remained standing there. Rather than get into his tent to pack, he took it down with his belongings still inside. He was going to have to tell the authorities about this, so he reached in for his camera, all the while keeping his eye on the figure on the slope above him. Having found his camera, he attempted to take a photo of the figure, but the figure threw another rock at him, putting him off that idea. He then reached in and pulled everything out to pack, while remaining alert for whatever was going on around him, and the figure on the hill. He packed as fast as he could, his tent last, shoving it in at the top of his rucksack rather than rolling it up properly. He heaved his rucksack onto his back and, with one last glance at the figure on the bluff, he headed towards the path back down to Rapadalen. Once he had a suitable distance from the figure, he turned to try again to take another photo, but the figure had vanished from the bluff. Noel had to get away from the figure and the boy as directly as he could. So he took the most immediate route back to the path, around the front of some steep rocks, adjacent to the drop down to the valley.

Noel continued round and came to a stretch of scree above the path. He needed to descend this, so he set off, struggling across it in the dark. He kept looking back as he went, but there was no-one. He still wished to continue his trek to Suorva, which would mean going back up towards the lake behind Låddebákte to camp there. But was it a realistic idea with these people around? Or these spirits? Whatever they were.

Slowly, Noel made his way down the slope and finally reached the path. He looked up and down it. There was no sign of anyone. It was darker now. The clouds had thickened and the moon was scarcely visible behind them. It was decision time. He was now a short distance below the top of the pass. Should he go back up there, and carry on on his original planned route? It wasn't very appealing with weather that looked like worsening and with mountain spirits up there. Otherwise he had to carry on down. But that suggested that he was giving up on the hike, and would have to head back to Aktse. There was a third option. That was to head to the hut at Skårkistugan and spend the night there, either in his tent, or if he could get in, in the hut. From there he could carry on up the Rapadalen valley, through the forest, and regain his original route further upstream. It seemed to make sense. There was no footpath on the map but that would mean that the area was little frequented, and might be good for wildlife sightings.

Noel crossed the gully that he had had to negotiate on the way up. His rucksack was giving him a lot of discomfort, badly packed as it was, and his neck was aching. From having felt so euphoric at the fabulous views he had experience up on Låddebákte, Noel was now feeling pretty miserable. This valley is so beautiful, he told himself, if only I could have understood that it had to be more than it seemed. As he reached the forest he noticed that it was starting to rain, quite big drops were hitting him. And with his torch he could see that there was snow mixed in with the rain. He stopped to affix a waterproof cover over his rucksack and started to look forward to reaching the hut at Skårkistugan.

Noel walked down through the forest, still on edge, but noticing nothing untoward. When he reached the valley floor, he saw the path turning off to the right, to the Skårkistugan hut, he assumed. He took the turning. It was close to midnight.

After about twenty yards, a fallen tree blocked the path. Usually where trees have fallen across paths, hikers establish a path around them. But Noel couldn't see any path here. Maybe the tree had fallen recently, so he clambered over it, struggling through the branches, and carried on. There were a lot of fallen trees along here. It didn't look as if it was a well-frequented path. Every tree that he had to climb over was awkward, especially in the dark and the sleet.

Noel turned a corner on the trail. In front of him, the path was blocked by fallen trees as far as he could see. How could this path be so bad? Had a storm come through here and blown all the trees over? Was it going to be like this all the way tomorrow as well? He could leave the path and go through the forest. There wouldn't be this many fallen trees that way. But then how would he find the hut in the middle of the forest if he wasn't on any sort of path? He had seen from his campsite up on Låddebákte just how deeply ensconced in the forest the hut was.

Noel looked again at the path ahead. He froze. There was somebody just standing there, in the middle of the fallen trees. The figure was looking down at the ground. Wearing some short of shaggy outfit, maybe made from reindeer skin. Noel didn't say anything, he just stood and stared. Slowly the figure raised his head to look back at Noel. The figure's face was bloodied and dirty. Noel couldn't face any more of this. The only way to walk now was back down the valley. It seemed as if the hike was now over. He was heading back to Aktse.

Was now an appropriate time to trigger the alarm on the ReachMe device? It was supposed to be for critical, life-threatening situations. This was certainly a critical situation. Noel was in an absolute crisis. He was being haunted by the illegitimate child and demons of Ähpár. Was it life-threatening? I don't know, thought Noel, I don't know if these demons take people's lives. Maybe they do, it goes with the territory. Isn't that what demons do? But if I trigger the alarm now, no-one is going to come until tomorrow. If I keep walking I could be close to Aktse by then. They can't land a helicopter in the trees. If I stay out here and camp somewhere where a helicopter can land, what kind of conversation do I have with the pilot tomorrow? That I triggered the alarm because I was being tormented by demons? He's going to think that I am crazy.

So Noel carried on down the path, nervously looking behind himself as he went. Was he going to keep walking all night until he got to Aktse? It was a possibility, albeit a miserable one. It was a long way. If he camped in the valley he was nervous of whomever it was that had interfered with his tent on the earlier occasion. The demon in the valley seemed more amenable than the ones up in the mountains, but was a demon nonetheless.

There was nothing to see as he walked. Just darkness and trees and the small area illuminated in front of him by his headtorch. It was much harder to follow the path from the light of his torch than it had been by daylight. The sleet kept falling, and the wind was blowing up the valley, into Noel's face. Because of the poor visibility, Noel kept having to stop and work out which way to go. Several times he lost the path and had to retrace his steps. He carried on. After a while, the sleet starting to turn to wet snow. It began sticking to his already wet waterproofs in a way that he had never experienced before. It started to form a thin layer of slush on them as it part-melted there. It wasn't easy to scrape off.

Noel would have got his map out to consider his options. But the map was in his rucksack and he would have to remove the waterproof cover which he had placed over the rucksack. It wasn't a very appealing prospect in the sleet and snow. Maybe he would look at it later, but for now his options were simple, either keep walking, through the night if necessary to Aktse, or veer off into the forest and camp somewhere. He wasn't entirely sure whether he had the courage to camp any longer.

Noel carried on, but it was miserable. He passed a small lake that he recalled from the way up, but mostly he had few visual indications of where he was. Just more trees. The melting snow was making its way through his waterproofs, and he was getting wet and cold. The melted snow was also getting into his boots. Things were going from bad to worse.

Noel reached a stream. His feet were already wet. Normally of course he would take his boots off to cross it, and then dry his feet off with his towel. But his feet were already wet and he would feel vulnerable, and get even colder, sitting down by the side of the stream to take his boots on and off. So he walked straight through. He hadn't thought that his feet could get any wetter. But now, instead of just being wet, they were also immersed in a mass of cold water swilling about in his boots. It was horrible.

As he continued, Noel's path took him close to the Ráhpaädno. The sound of its rushing waters in the darkness was frightening. Noel looked at them with his headtorch. All that cold energy, carrying on, through the night. It seemed sinister compared to how the river had looked by day. The idea even crossed his mind of just throwing himself in, to put an end to all this discomfort and suffering. He was getting really cold, wet, and his feet were hurting. The path just seemed to go on forever. It seemed interminable.

Noel walked on, getting ever colder. It didn't make sense for him to keep going all night to Aktse. It would just be too miserable an experience. He had camped in the forest once before and not been disturbed. He would do so now. He veered off into the forest, stumbled through and over fallen trees, until he found a secluded spot where he could not see why anyone would possibly be able to find him. He then put his tent up as quietly as possible, checking around that no-one was watching him. He got into the tent, sat down with his feet out in the lobby, took his boots off, poured the water out of them with abjection, got changed into some dry clothes and into his sleeping bag. It was 2:30a.m.

In the relief of the relative safety of his tent, and warmth of his sleeping bag, Noel's emotions overcame him. He broke down, sobbing. He didn't feel as if he could take this any more. Had he really seen what he thought he had seen up on Låddebákte and at Skårkistugan? Was he having hallucinations? Was he losing his sanity? He didn't know. Who was doing this to him? Should he have just carried on beyond Låddebákte instead of returning back down the valley? No. It was further and more remote that way, and he just had to get out of this situation now. But his trip was ruined.

So he lay there, his sobbing slowly subsiding. He was terrified of being disturbed again. All that he could do was to stay in his tent and hope that nothing happened. If something did happen now, he didn't know if he would have the strength to do anything about it. His was emotionally exhausted and he didn't know if he would have the reserves to defend himself. The next time anything happened, he decided, he would trigger the emergency alarm. He would explain that he had done so because he had been getting hypothermic and was starting to have hallucinations. No need to mention any demons to anyone. If he had to pay for the rescue, or if he looked an idiot, he didn't care.

*

Noel must eventually have fallen asleep. But he found himself awake. There was a smell. He inhaled a couple of times to check it. It was unmistakeable. It was petrol fumes. Had his stove somehow got turned on? He hadn't removed it from his rucksack. It shouldn't have done. He reached for his torch so that he could find his stove to check it. As he did so, something hard hit his tent. It seemed as if it was a rock. Somebody was out there. This nightmare looked like it was never going to end. He had to get out of his tent. He grabbed a trekking pole to defend himself, and rushed out. As he got out of the tent, another rock came. He stood up to try to look where it had come from. There was some movement in the trees. But then another projectile came, but this one was in flames! It struck the side of his tent, and in an instant the whole tent was ablaze. He heard someone running off in the darkness. He screamed and swore at whomever it was. But it was useless to follow – he was barefoot and didn't have his headtorch.

Noel grabbed a fallen branch, and beat the flames down. The tent burnt so quickly that within a few moments there was nothing left of it. Just his tent poles stood there, blackened. His other possessions were there, still in what remained of the tent, singed, but for the most part unburnt. A charred bottle lay on the ground, close to what was left of his tent. Clearly that was the source of the ignition. What the hell was going on? He just wanted to break down and cry. Was someone trying to kill him? Presumably not, or they wouldn't have thrown the rocks, they would have just set the tent on fire with him inside. Maybe that was some mercy. But it meant that the only thing for him now was to try to get out of the mountains, to safety. How on earth did they find him wherever he went? He scanned around in the forest with his headtorch, but, as he expected there was no sign of anyone. Whoever it was could have gone some distance by now.

The situation had clearly become an emergency. Noel got out the ReachMe, opened the cover flap, and gave the S.O.S. button a long, hard press. The alarm gave a series of flashing lights to indicate that it was sending the alert, and determining his GPS position. From what Noel could see, the unit was working as expected. The Swedish authorities should be notified promptly. He understood that the ReachMe would now start transmitting his position to the authorities every five minutes. So if he were to continue hiking out, he could still be found. That was what he would have to do. He couldn't stay where he was all night in the wet snow without a tent. He would get too cold. All he could do was to pack his things up as best he could, and try to be in a suitable place for a helicopter to land to collect him at dawn. He took a few photos of his tent, as a record of what had happened, and set off.

## VI

Stephen Kendale was at his desk at the Government Communications Headquarters (GCHQ) in Cheltenham, England. He received notification on his computer that Noel had triggered the alarm on his ReachMe device. The ReachMe was sold and operated by a company, Outdoor Tracking Services Limited, based in Basingstoke, about 40 miles outside of London. Ordinarily, Outdoor Tracking Services would handle all notifications sent through the ReachMe. However, Stephen had received a warrant authorising interception of communications made by Noel's ReachMe. He had diverted all communications from the ReachMe to come directly to him. Outdoor Tracking Services would not have been aware that Noel had triggered his alarm, and the Swedish authorities would not be notified. Only at such time as Stephen might decide to forward the message on would they be informed.

To explain the development of the ReachMe it is necessary to go back some time before Noel's hike. The Coronavirus outbreak of 2020 had changed society forever. The initial outbreak had caused society to be locked down, and much economic activity to be suspended. Vaccines were developed, and they were always effective in bringing the number of cases down, but it seemed to keep happening that, after a few months, just as it looked appropriate to open society up again, a new strain of the virus would take hold, and the lockdowns would be extended a bit further. There were occasional interludes when bars and restaurants would open, and when foreign travel was possible. But for most of the time, little was possible, and people shopped online and, to the extent that they still worked, did so online.

Of course, with so little economic activity taking place, there was a problem of how people would have sufficient income to live on. The essential activities, producing and distributing food to the population and providing medical care, could only occupy so many people. With so many leisure facilities closed, there was a risk of huge unemployment. So the UK government agreed that employers could furlough employees and it would then pay their wages. Of course, like the lockdowns, these furlough arrangements were always temporary when announced. But they always got renewed.

So where did the government get all the money from to make all these furlough payments? To start with, it wasn't just the furlough payments that had to be financed. There was also a welter of loans which the government gave to businesses to keep them afloat. The total annual cost ran into many billions of pounds. The answer as to where the government got the money from was that the government sold debt, in the form of bonds, on the money markets, to banks. Why were the banks happy to buy so much debt? Because they were confident that the Bank of England would buy it off them, and they would make a small profit on the transaction. Why did the Bank of England buy it? Supposedly it was for "quantitative easing", to stimulate the economy. Certainly it would be good if the economy could be stimulated. But how could it make sense to talk about stimulating the economy if everyone was locked down at home? What element of the economy was actually going to be stimulated? The fact that the amount of bonds bought each month by the Bank of England was a close match to the government's borrowing requirements led many to the conclusion that the Bank of England was simply funding the government, and that its actions were nothing really to do with quantitative easing. Where did the Bank of England get the money from? It just printed it. Not literally, but all it had to do was write up its creation in a ledger. How would the government repay the money that it was borrowing, with so many people not working and tax receipts accordingly so low? Were people on furlough, or loan-aided businesses, going to pay the government more in taxes than they received from the government? Obviously not. No-one had any idea how the government would repay the money. Maybe it never would. Maybe the Bank of England would just write it off. But in any case there was a general agreement, from all political parties, as well as the Bank of England, that this scheme of arrangements was the appropriate way forward. Otherwise a lot of people simply wouldn't have enough money to live on.

The furlough arrangements helped, but were not sufficient to stop unemployment from climbing. Furloughed employees reaching retirement age had no reason to retire, and employers were unable (and had no reason) to oblige them to do so, the Default Retirement Age having been abolished some years earlier. There was never any reason for employers to make employees redundant either – it would cost them money to do so, whereas keeping them on, on furlough, did not.

The big problem with all of this, of course, was that, while there was no reason for employers to terminate any employment, there was also no reason for them to create any new jobs. What was the point of employing someone, only to immediately put them on furlough? But in the UK, 700,000 young people were coming onto the jobs market every year. And many of them couldn't find jobs. A lot of employers who would normally take them on weren't creating any new positions. This naturally created intense resentment. Young people were finding that their lives were in a state of permanent limbo. Once they had finished their studies (online) there was often little to do but claim unemployment benefit, and stay at home with their parents. There was a huge sense of injustice that many older people were being paid a reasonable wage to do nothing, while younger people were obliged to sign on for unemployment benefits and look for jobs that really there was no reason to expect them to be able to find.

After a few years, the resentment felt by young people, as they felt excluded from the furlough arrangements, started to spill over. Street protests had for a long time been illegal because of the risk of spreading the virus through contact between protestors. Quite a few protests had nonetheless taken place in the earlier days of the pandemic, largely against the lockdown restrictions. People had felt that there was no way that the police could issue fines against everyone at the protest, and had been prepared to take the risk of being fined themselves, considering that the chances were low. There was some discussion of allowing protests while continuing to allow other gatherings. But the government rightly felt that that would be abused. If it were to allow protests, then what was to stop anyone holding a gathering claiming that it was a protest. If what you really wanted was to hold a large picnic then wouldn't you just paint some banners and leave them around your picnic site and claim that it was a protest? Would there have to be some sort of list of appropriate subjects to protest against, or could the protest be about anything, say the lack of strawberries in the supermarkets? Or the weather? It seemed unworkable, and the government decided to maintain its ban on protests. In spite of the ban, they continued, and, where the protestors had thought they had some immunity from the police by virtue of their numbers, they were sadly proved wrong, as had happened in many other parts of the world before. The government felt that its only option was to authorise the use of tear gas and water cannon by the police. People were horrified, but the measures worked. Street protests were virtually eliminated.

Young, unemployed people, frustrated by their lives going nowhere, started to think of another way to protest however. If they could make a quick demonstration, and get away very quickly, that would be very hard for the government to control. The police would never be able to attend in time. The obvious tool for this form of protest was the bicycle. Lacking any means of identification, and quick to get around the streets, bicycles met requirements very well. So a new type of protest started to develop. Cyclists would turn up *en masse* overnight at government buildings. They organised themselves online to do this. They would leave banners with messages such as "Furlough for All Now" on the buildings, then quickly disappear. The original meaning of the word "furlough" was getting lost – it was coming to mean simply a right to be paid for not doing anything.

Initially the bicycle protests didn't attract much attention. The banners would be quickly cleared up by the authorities in the morning and there would be little or no press coverage. So unfortunately, to attract more attention, the protestors started to get violent. They would all appear at the same time, outside a government building in the middle of the night, and would then unleash a volley of fireworks, open paint pots and other missiles at it, then rapidly disperse. Sometimes they would also steal whatever they could – things such as plants and plaques on the buildings. The police would of course race to the scene, but it was very difficult (a) for them to approach closely with all the projectiles being launched and (b) to catch more than a handful of the perpetrators of each attack, if any, because they would all cycle off in different directions. Cyclists were careful to ensure that they did not have any incriminating evidence on them as they cycled away in case they were intercepted as they cycled home. And they did what they could to remove any identifying features from their bicycles. If they were intercepted by the police they would claim that they were just out for some late-night exercise, finding it safer to cycle when no-one else was around, from the point of view of catching the virus. Come the morning the building would be a mess, and clear messages demanding furlough for everyone would be prominently visible. It was successful in getting the protestors the attention that they wanted for their cause.

The government was of course horrified by this new development. Its initial reaction to these protests was to impose a curfew. After all, there was little need for anyone to be out in the middle of the night with all night-time venues closed because of the pandemic. So henceforth, no-one was allowed out between 9p.m. and 6a.m. But the response of the protestors was simply to switch to carrying out the protests during the day. In some ways it worked better. Cyclists could approach the building and carry out the attack wearing a helmet and facemask. It meant that they would not be recognisable later and there was certainly nothing suspicious about a cyclist wearing a helmet and facemask. After the attack cyclists could simply stop off at a nearby supermarket, do some shopping, and cycle home with their purchases. The police simply needed to hear that they had gone out to do some shopping.

Of course, the police started to stop and search cyclists with rucksacks to see if they were carrying any projectiles. They arrested a few cyclists who were carrying fireworks, and before long the use of fireworks almost completely stopped. But the protestors got very skilled at merging their attacks in with shopping trips, and carried on much as before, using items such as bleach, paint, tomatoes, and flammable liquids disguised in drinks bottles. The development was becoming one of grave concern to the government. It asserted that it had made available payments of billions of pounds for furlough payments, and that, while it regretted the situation that a lot of young people were in, it was simply not appropriate to make furlough payments for jobs that did not actually exist. A comment by one government minister that there was "no magic money tree" to make payments enraged protestors. It was clear that there was a magic money tree for making furlough payments to older people, but not for them.

The police had an additional tactic at their disposal. This was to try to infiltrate the protestors' networks. The protestors organised themselves through social media groups where they would announce the targets of their protests around an hour before the designated time. The police would authorise agents to form relationships with the protestors, and try to gain access to their online groups. Their job was then to find out who the organisers were, determine information about the planned protests, and to tip the police off. The technical term for these infiltrators is "covert human intelligence sources", or CHISs. CHISs could be authorised if it were considered necessary to prevent crime or disorder, as was the case here. The CHISs would infiltrate the social media groups, posing as potential demonstrators themselves, and they would also attend protests, in order to appear genuine to the other members of the groups. If they failed to show up and take part in protests, their identity would be suspect, and they would be at risk of being excluded, and so unable to obtain any useful information. The police had quite a significant amount of success in prosecuting the ringleaders of the attacks with this tactic.

There was one problem for the CHISs in entering the social media groups and attending the protests, and that was that technically they were often committing criminal acts themselves. They were breaching curfews, gathering in breach of lockdown laws, and committing criminal damage, and conspiring to do all of that by their involvement in the groups. So by carrying out their role they were putting themselves at risk of being charged with criminal acts. This was naturally a discouragement to anyone prepared to take on a role as a CHIS – they wanted some confirmation that they weren't going to be prosecuted for doing what the police had asked them to do, and it was quite a reasonable demand that they should have some protection from that.

This issue had been considered in new legislation - The Covert Human Intelligence Sources (Criminal Conduct) Act 2021[1]. This enabled a CHIS to benefit from what was known as a "criminal conduct authorisation" (CCA). This authorisation would grant him immunity from prosecution for specified criminal offences which might be carried out in the course of his role as a CHIS. Having authorised a CHIS, Government bodies, including the police, could then grant a CCA to the CHIS. The CCAs could be made on the grounds of preventing or detecting crime or disorder, as with the CHIS authorisations.

The criminal conduct authorisations had to specify the criminal acts which they authorised. The person granting the CCA could not authorise anything that would cause an individual's human rights, as set out in the Human Rights Act, to be breached. So this did at least prevent the authorisation of murder, torture, submitting an individual to inhuman or degrading treatment, and deprivation of his liberty. Depriving an individual of his possessions was not permitted under the Human Rights Act unless it was in the public interest or otherwise authorised by the law. That was OK then, it could be authorised under the CCA and could be argued to be in the public interest because it was to prevent disorder. So the CCAs were usually drafted to allow the CHISs to breach curfew regulations, assemble in public in breach of social distancing regulations, commit affray, criminal damage and theft (because some objects were being stolen from outside the government offices), and to conspire to and aid and abet each of these.

There was an additional requirement that criminal conduct authorisations had to be notified to a Judicial Commissioner

---

[1] See the Appendix

(essentially a judge taking submissions from only one party), as soon as possible or in any event within seven days of granting the authorisation. The notification had to set out the grounds on which the authorising person was authorising the criminal conduct, and list the crimes which were authorised. The Judicial Commissioner did not have the power to annul the authorisation, but would give details of it to the Investigatory Powers Commissioner who would produce an annual report on how the legislation was working.

As mentioned, the original justification given for introducing the legislation around criminal conduct authorisations was to protect CHISs from criminal charges arising out of the activities which were integral to their role as CHISs. But, as enacted, the legislation didn't say that. It did not say that the criminal conduct had to be necessary for protecting the source. Instead it simply said that it had to be in the course of or in connection with the CHIS operation. So, given that criminal damage and theft were authorised, some CHIS and police who authorised them started to see an opportunity to expand the role by having these crimes committed not to protect the source, but to intimidate the people being surveyed. This could be effective in achieving the aims of the operation, to prevent disorder, surely? So it began to happen that cyclists would have their homes broken into and vandalised, bicycles stolen and bricks being thrown through their windows. No doubt some were engaged in protests, but many were probably completely innocent. They would report the incidents to the police, but the police, on establishing that a criminal conduct authorisation was in place, would simply respond that it would not be in the public interest to take the matter further. The reason it would not be in the public interest was of course that any prosecution would fail because of the CCA. Finally, one aggrieved cyclist was able to identify the person who had vandalised his bicycle. The police refused to take any action, so he brought a private prosecution. When it finally came to light that the culprit had the benefit of a criminal conduct authorisation, and so could not be prosecuted, there was outrage. It seemed as if the government had taken to just retaliating in kind against those whom it suspected of crimes. It seemed as if the government found this much more expedient than prosecuting criminal suspects through the courts. Pay for criminal lawyers had fallen year on year, and delays of several years in criminal cases coming to court were the norm. There just wasn't the will to use the court system any more, when it was so much easier and cheaper for the government just to retaliate in kind. But of course, this meant that the government had sunk to a level where it had no better moral authority than ordinary criminals. Unsurprisingly, further spontaneous protests followed.

Eventually the government gave way on the furlough issue. Partly this was because it couldn't deny that the system was unfair. But it was also because of the advent of a new political party, by which it felt threatened. This was the Reality Party. The traditional political parties seemed to have come to agreement on the appropriate level of government spending, i.e. very large, and decided that their position had moved enough. But they had seemed to shut out the idea of more widespread furlough payments. The Reality Party advocated this. But it was also concerned about a lot of other social injustices, including ones of more traditional concern such as racial, gender and disability inequalities. It was determined to put an end to them, and part of its strategy was "wokeism". If you didn't agree with its views then you were not "woke", and were therefore out of touch, offensive and irrelevant. That was the end of the matter. It was an *ad hominem* argument, but *ad hominem* arguments were starting to be the order of the day.

So the government decided to create the "Furlough in Action" scheme, whereby employers could take on new staff to be furloughed from the outset. This reduced unemployment, and supposedly it meant that there would be more jobs in existence for when the economy finally recovered. In order to encourage employers to take on furloughed staff, the government paid them a modest fee, to cover the administrative costs, and they were happy to oblige. The employers would usually provide some video training for the newly-recruited furloughed employees to watch in order to be fully trained for when the situation finally returned to normal. With furlough now available to more people, the protests started to subside, but the fact that they had occurred left a bitter taste in the government's mouth.

In 1928, the economist John Maynard Keynes had written a short essay entitled "Economic Possibilities for Our Grandchildren". In it, he suggested that the "economic problem", the problem of securing the basic human requirements for subsistence, would be solved within 100 years. Technological advances would be such that people would need to work only a few hours a day, or not at all. Technological advances did of course continue after 1928. So looking at it from a 1920s perspective, surely less labour was needed, and people could work less, or even not at all? But there was a problem in that. How would people pay for their subsistence requirements if they were not working? Where would they get the money from? It seemed wasteful and irresponsible for the government to simply give them money. But the virus had led to governments doing just that. People were being given money without having to work for it. The sum situation that had come about was that central banks were printing money, nominally to buy government bonds to support the economy, but seemingly in reality just to finance the government. The government was paying this money to people to do jobs that they held, but never actually had to do. The money was flowing from the Bank of England to individuals. The government owned the Bank of England. So the government was now printing money to give people the life of leisure promised by Keynes. It had taken almost exactly 100 years, as suggested by Keynes. But the way that it had come about, and was presented, was something that he could not possibly have imagined. The pill had also been made easier to swallow by the idea that it was temporary, although of course it was not, because it kept being extended. It had taken a virus, and the bicycle, to finally crack the Keynesian conundrum.

Several years after the start of the pandemic, credited by much of the electorate with having helped resolve the furlough issue, the Reality Party came to power.

## VII

As the years went by, people started to resign themselves to simpler pleasures than they had known in the past. Cycling, open water swimming and walking were all popular. Some foreign travel was possible, although if you were to avoid a lengthy quarantine at either end you had to be sure that the country you were visiting did not consider your country to be a risk, and vice versa for the return trip. Of course it was an ever-changing situation, but websites were set up where you could register your home country and list countries you were interested in travelling to, and whenever there was a clear possibility of making a trip, the website would send you an email to let you know. Still, the problem with going abroad now was that experience often wasn't really that special. At the destination, access to beaches might be limited, tourist attractions closed and evening entertainment subject to curfew. Holidaymakers might just be swapping restrictions at home for restrictions abroad. It hardly seemed worth the trouble.

One way that some people did find to have a more fulfilling holiday was simply to take a tent and go backpacking out in the wilderness. Once you were away from civilisation you could observe nature, do some sketching, take photos, go wild swimming, whatever. You actually had freedom for once without the ever-present worry of virus-related restrictions. There would be no officials around who might impose sudden quarantine requirements on you. And certainly no-one could argue that you weren't self-isolating. So people would sometimes just disappear into the wilderness for a week or more, limited only by how much food they could carry. But some hikers took it further. Who was going to check if you were actually social distancing if you were deep inside a remote forest somewhere? Some people took to camping in large groups for weeks on end in out of the way places. Again, encrypted Internet chat rooms meant that these gatherings could be organised without the authorities becoming aware of their existence. Solo hikers would walk in from different directions and meet up for a week of partying in a pre-arranged location. The discovery of a summer encampment holding in excess of a hundred people from all over Europe, deep in a mountain forest in Bulgaria, complete with sound system, bar, and dining facilities, set alarm bells ringing in many governments. It was clearly no sort of social isolation. How many of these camps were there across Europe?

The response of governments was to make a complete review of the arrangements around people heading into wilderness areas. Some countries began drone patrols to search for illegal gatherings. Once a drone found a gathering, it would take photos, and enforcement officials would normally make their way in to disperse the gathering and issue fines. But of course it took time for them to get there, and people had often dispersed by the time they arrived. Still of course it had the desired effect of discouraging the gatherings.

Even people hiking in groups was not really desirable, unless they were all from the same household. Commercial guided hiking tours had had to cease their activities early on in the pandemic; with participants coming from a lot of different places, the risk of spreading the virus on these trips was evident. In order to encourage people to hike in smaller groups, the British government had set up Outdoor Tracking Services Limited, and developed the ReachMe, the device which Noel carried. The government made the ReachMe available at a very affordable price to hikers in order to give people the confidence to hike alone since this would encourage social isolation. Indeed it had become quite common for people to take lengthy backpacking trips through the remotest parts of Europe with one of these devices for security, and to do so alone, as Noel was doing, or in a couple. Social isolation, even extreme social isolation, had

74

become rather fashionable. The effect of this was notable in the area where Noel was hiking. In the past a 270-mile trail, known as the Kungsleden, used to run north-south through the Swedish mountains, passing through Aktse, and east of the Sarek National Park. It had been very popular both in summer for hikers, and winter, for skiers and snowmobilers. It was well-maintained and marked. But hiking it was not a way to practise social isolation, as hikers would inevitably pass many others, and liked to stop in the same places overnight. So people had been encouraged to switch to hiking more in the style that Noel was doing. The Kungsleden had fallen into disuse.

So it was not particularly unusual that Noel was undertaking his solo hike. But the new popularity of undertaking remote hikes is really just an incidental part of the explanation.

Noel had worked for the last twelve years for UK Visas and Immigration, a part of the Home Office. He worked in a large 1970s office block in Croydon, south London. Much of his work was concerned with handling asylum cases. There was a steady flow of asylum seekers coming to Britain in spite of the pandemic, with many arriving having crossed the English Channel in inflatable dinghies. The asylum seekers inhabited a different world to everyone else so far as the virus was concerned. If obliged to quarantine in a hotel on arrival they didn't particularly mind, and they certainly didn't pay for it – they couldn't. If fined for a breach of social distancing regulations, again, they were never going to pay. And it was often impossible for the government to send them back to their country of origin, because the UK had its own strains of the virus which often caused those other countries to prohibit entry to anyone who had been in the UK. So largely the asylum-seekers did as they pleased. They continued to arrive, and Noel remained very busy. In fact the hours had got ever longer as a result of government cuts and increased paperwork in his job. Although he worked largely online from home, he was having to carry out ever more asylum interviews, and there were interminable meetings with other Home Office Officials to attend. He was actually working about an eighty-hour week. Like everything, it was a temporary situation which seemed to go on forever. There was always some crisis to justify it.

Noel also felt great dissatisfaction in his job because of positive discrimination measures which had been implemented by the Reality Party. All companies and government authorities had been obliged to employ a specific number of women, members of ethnic and other minorities to the more senior positions. This was achieved by means of an algorithm, produced by a panel of diversity experts from a number of universities with well-regarded expertise in that field. It seemed fairly obvious that this algorithm was very discriminatory, particularly against white, middle-class men such as Noel. But how can you argue with an algorithm? Noel felt that this discrimination was behind his lack of progress at work, and that he was being marginalised there. Further, his evident unhappiness made him an easy target for bullying. In the weekly online departmental meeting which he attended his bosses would make little comments designed to humiliate him – "what does Noel think about this?" as if his opinion was just of interest for entertainment purposes, "the practical side of things has never really been quite your *forte*, has it Noel?", "never really did fit in here, did you Noel?". He was miserable.

What action could he take? He submitted a complaint through the Home Office's internal complaints system. But he didn't feel that it was taken seriously. The Home Secretary was one of the Reality Party's most wokeist MPS, and he had instigated a culture of wokeism that extended throughout the whole organisation. The determination made by the complaints committee seemed to place most of the blame for the situation on Noel. It said that his filing of the complaint suggested a poor understanding of the importance of diversity. He considered simply resigning, and claiming constructive dismissal, and bringing a claim to an employment tribunal. But why should that be much different to following the internal complaints procedure? And would he ever be able to get another job after taking such a step? He would have trouble claiming benefits if he was found to have resigned without good reason, and the determination made by the complaints committee would certainly work against him in that regard.

As a civil servant Noel was not entitled to express his political opinions publicly without approval from his line manager. He wrote an article attacking the use of the diversity algorithm and asked for approval to publish it, but this was denied. The grounds given were that the algorithm had been developed by the most highly-regarded experts on these matters. It was also commented that Noel, in his article had concerningly demonstrated an "almost total lack of self-awareness regarding diversity issues." He was made to take part in a diversity training course, again increasing his hours. More humiliating comments were forthcoming in departmental meetings.

One night Noel was lying in bed, unable to sleep, having conducted an asylum interview late that evening. An intriguing thought came to him. He spent all of his days thinking about whether people were being persecuted, and had ground for asylum. What if, in fact, he was being persecuted? If he were an asylum seeker he would say that he was discriminated against on the grounds of his gender, race and sexual orientation. Maybe also because of his political beliefs – that he believed that the diversity quotas were inappropriate. The effect of this discrimination was that he was unable to pursue a private life. He was working all the time to the point where he had no life. And there was no way that he could realistically hope to support a family on his salary. If he had been promoted then that would have been less the case. So the discrimination that he was suffering was having the effect of breaching his human rights, and severely so. He had sought protection from his employer and it hadn't helped. He was not comfortable about taking the matter to court. His situation met all the requirements for claiming asylum. How ironic that he spent all his time helping asylum seekers flee persecution when he in fact was in a similar situation to them. How would he look on his claim if he was assessing it? He would probably have to accept it actually. He kept thinking about it until he fell asleep.

*

Noel woke up very early, well before his alarm clock went off. His idea from last night, claiming asylum, was still in his head. He couldn't claim asylum in his own country, so, if he did it, where would go? Sweden seemed the obvious choice. A country that he had been to before, and liked, and one with a tradition of accepting asylum seekers. It would be an insane thing for him to do. But the logic stood up. He would have to show that he was being persecuted in the UK and that his human rights were being breached. He felt that he could make a fair case for it. He would have to start a new life in Sweden, but it would certainly be a way to make his point. There would probably be a lot of press interest. Crazy though the idea seemed, he was really starting to warm to the idea of doing it. That was it. He would do it. He really was going to do it. He was going to go to Sweden. As a refugee.

Noel couldn't help but smile as he contemplated actually carrying out his plan. In all truth, he wouldn't miss Croydon. Why not take a gamble on starting afresh in Sweden? He didn't know how life in Sweden would be, but he was certain to have a lot of new experiences there. Was there really that much to lose?

What if, though, just to pull things back a bit, he went hiking again in Sweden first to think it over? Then if he still really wanted to claim asylum, he could do so after the hike? That made more sense than going straight there to do it. Yes, that's what he would do. A week or two's hiking, then down to Stockholm and put in his claim there. He laughed to himself at the extraordinariness of his plan. He would hike alone, he was OK with that. But what a sensation! A British person claiming asylum in Sweden. It should create quite a stir. He felt genuinely excited by the idea.

That day, Noel put in a request for annual leave at work, which was approved. Later that evening he began researching his trip online. It was early September so he did not have long before it would get too cold for his hike. But he had enough time. He already had all of the equipment that he needed, but he ordered a map, a lot of dehydrated food, booked transport arrangements, and made a post on HikeBackCountry.com to ask for advice about his planned route. With regard to his possessions, he decided that he would pack them up and put them in storage. He didn't have too many. He made a reservation with a storage company and they confirmed that he would be able to remove his possessions and have them sent to him at his expense at a later date if he so wished.

Noel also read up on obtaining asylum in Sweden, although, being familiar with arrangements for this in the UK, there was not that much that was new. He noted that he could do this in Stockholm, Gothenburg, Malmö and the inland town of Örebro. Örebro was clearly the smallest city, and that seemed appealing. He liked the idea of being a bit more out of the way when he made his application, and accommodation would probably be cheaper. It also had a wonderful-looking castle, which he could spend some time looking around. That was where he would go. He booked a train ticket, and hotel accommodation close to the migration office.

## VIII

Noel's immediate superior at work was a Senior Officer in UK Visas and Immigration, a lady by the name of Sally Krosen. Noel didn't like her. She was dry and humourless, and he resented the fact that she was younger than him. Some months before his decision to travel to Sweden she had sought, on the grounds of his impaired diversity thinking, and obtained, approval to monitor his personal Internet browsing.

Sally was interested to know what Noel's holiday plans were, so she had a look at his browsing history. She could see that he had booked a flight to Arlanda Airport, and train travel from there up to the Arctic. She could see his train trip for after the hike which took him to Örebro. There was no sign of a flight back home. He had also booked a hotel in this town for three nights, taking him beyond the date he was due back at work. What on earth was he going to Örebro for? Sally looked up some details about the town. OK, it was something of a tourist destination, but that didn't explain why he was planning to stay there beyond the date when he was due back in the office. She did some more research and discovered, piquing her interest further, that there was an office of the Swedish Migration Agency at Örebro. She could see that Noel had also been looking at the website of the Swedish Migration Agency. What was this, some sort of busman's tour? She decided to call Noel up, on video.

"I see you're off on holiday?" she asked

"Yes. I wanted to squeeze something in before the summer was over."

"Going somewhere nice?"

"Yes, I've decided to go to Sweden again."

"More hiking I suppose."

"Yes. There's another area I'd like to explore. Should be beautiful."

"Are you going anywhere else while you're there?"

"No, just hiking."

Noel was clearly lying, but Sally couldn't let on that she knew.

"Well, I'm sure we'll manage without you. What day are you due back … let me see … 3rd October. Don't be late, will you? That backlog is only getting worse."

"No, I'll be back then." There was nothing in Noel's demeanour to give away the fact that he had any plans otherwise, although Sally knew that he did.

"Are you just going by yourself?"

"Yep."

"Out in the wilds the whole time. Not going to enjoy a bit of city life?" continued Sally, fishing further.

"No, I get enough of the city while I'm here thanks," replied Noel.

"Well, you're very brave, is all I can say. Don't come to any harm while you're there. Rather you than me."

This was extremely concerning to Sally. It didn't look as if Noel was planning to be back at work on time, and he was clearly lying about it. In spite of what he said, he was going to Örebro for at least three nights. What on earth was he planning? Sally found another search that Noel had made online. It was simply "Has a British person ever claimed asylum?" So was that it, was he going to go to Örebro to claim asylum? Was he crazy? How could he possibly claim asylum? Sally reflected that Noel had made some complaints about how he felt he was being mistreated at work. In one outburst he had in fact suggested that his failure to get a promotion for so long was due to his lack of diversity. He said he was being discriminated against. Of course it was nonsense. But could that be grounds for claiming asylum? It seemed extreme, but if it meant that he felt his human rights were being breached, maybe he really was going to make such a claim. Sally started to feel that claiming asylum was what he really was going to do.

And the more Sally thought about it, the more she hated the prospect. Not simply that her department would be even more short-staffed, but what if, as a boss, she had an employee claiming asylum? Such an unusual step would be sure to capture the interest of the press, and she would look terrible. She could see the headline in a tabloid newspaper now. They would get a photo of her leaving the office, and print, above it something like: "Is this the WORST boss in the world? She bullied one of her employees to the point where he claimed ASYLUM!!!". The prospect was just too awful.

Sally thought about it further. She could find nothing to shake her from her conviction that Noel was going to claim asylum. What could she do to prevent it? She couldn't prevent him from taking a holiday; it had already been granted, he was overdue holiday, and he had made a lot of arrangements for it. Could she speak to him to try to dissuade him? It would be very difficult if he was just going to deny that he had such plans as he had. Could she give him the long-awaited promotion, and hope that that would appease him? No, a promotion would entail a pay rise, and there were no funds available. And she wasn't sure that the algorithm would allow it. Could he somehow be intimidated not to do this? It was hard to think what form that intimidation might take. She couldn't do anything illegal.

Or, on second thoughts, maybe she could do something illegal. There was a mechanism designed expressly for it. A criminal conduct authorisation. If it was in the news that a British person was claiming asylum in Sweden on the grounds that he felt bullied and discriminated against by a government department, wouldn't that create a risk of public disorder? The Visa and Immigration offices had been attacked in a protest just a couple of months ago. It might well happen again if this got out. So, logically, to prevent disorder, Sally could authorise someone to commit illegal acts to intimidate Noel into not claiming asylum. That person would have to become a CHIS in order to be granted a criminal conduct authorisation. But there must be a way to arrange that. It did all seem to add up.

The basis on which the Covert Human Intelligence Sources (Criminal Conduct) Act had initially been proposed was that the need for the CHIS would arise first, and then the criminal conduct authorisation would be provided to enable the CHIS to carry out whatever crimes were needed to maintain his cover. But nowhere did it say that it actually had to be like that. There was nothing to stop the logic from actually being the other way round. The public authority could think of the crimes that it wanted to commit first, and then think of a way to have a CHIS, so that the crimes could be authorised. And that suited Sally down to the ground.

So what Sally needed was someone to be up in the Arctic while Noel was there, and to intimidate him. That person would enter into some sort of relationship with Noel in order to be a CHIS and would benefit from a criminal conduct authorisation. She knew a man who she thought could help. His name was Matt Elkins. He was a former Royal Marine, now working freelance in CHIS operations for a range of government departments. He had trained in Arctic Norway, and was very familiar with the topography of northern Scandinavia, where Noel was going, albeit having had experience mostly in the winter rather than in the autumn. She would give him a call. But first she wanted to gain a little more understanding of the legalities of CCAs. There was an in-house lawyer in the office, and she could talk to her about it. Her name was Angela Speight. Angela had prepared a CCA and CHIS authorisation for Sally once before, in relation to a people-smuggling operation from Belgium into the UK. But Sally was not going to ask her to get involved in this current matter. Angela would ask questions, she would obviously be struck by how different this case was to the usual investigations into customs fraud and people-smuggling that they carried out, and if she found out that the subject of the investigation and CCA was an employee of UK Visas and Immigration, that would really take some explaining on Sally's part. So Sally thought she would just probe Angela for information in the most general manner possible and then handle the matter herself. She called Angela up and arranged to meet for lunch in the office canteen that day.

At lunch, the conversation came around to the recent people-smuggling investigation.

"You know how, in Belgium, we got a CCA for our man there," related Sally, "What I didn't understand was, if that was ever going to really help. I mean, if he had been arrested by the Belgian police for being involved in a people-smuggling operation, would they really pay much heed when he says he's got a criminal conduct authorisation from the UK?"

"Well, yes, indeed!" replied Angela, with a laugh. "I think the police would just say 'wot iz zis?'" She mimicked, holding up a piece of paper while making a puzzled look. She continued, supressing a smile, "But, even if it's not going to work, if it keeps our source happy, then it's achieved something!" Sally laughed.

"But actually, more seriously," continued Angela, "there are good reasons for it. Firstly, since the Domestic Abuse Act was passed a few years ago, quite a few offences have been prosecutable in the UK even when carried out abroad. That used to just be the case for murder and manslaughter. But now it's been extended to quite a few other things such as assault, harassment and stalking."

"But hang on, this has nothing to do with domestic abuse."

"Well that's the way laws work sometimes. What they actually do sometimes goes a lot further than the title. A cynic might suggest that that it's done so that they get less scrutiny in Parliament than they otherwise might. That's the way of the world. Anyway, the CCA should work to prevent prosecution in the UK under that Act of crimes committed abroad. So it's helpful there. Secondly, there's the issue of extradition. If the Belgians were to make an extradition request of our man, I think that the CCA would probably work to block it. If a country requests extradition of someone for something that wouldn't be a crime in their own country, then the extradition won't be granted. The CCA means that what would have been a crime had it been committed in the UK, in fact wasn't one, so no extradition is possible. In theory. Or maybe the CCA means that the crime was still a crime, but it was simply an authorised crime. And in that case, perhaps the source can still be extradited. Which would be a great shame. But obviously you don't mention that to your source, do you?"

"No, indeed. So it seems to be a similar situation with the CCA legislation as your Domestic Abuse Act. The bill was promoted on the basis that criminal conduct would be authorised to allow CHISs to maintain their cover. But what it actually says is that criminal conduct can be authorised to prevent disorder and crime."

"Yes, it is so."

"But how did that come about? Aren't there checks in place to prevent that? Didn't the Act have to go through the Houses of Commons and Lords to get approved first?"

"Well, firstly there's no knowing whether it was by accident or design. The Bill was sponsored by the Home Office and officials here would have worked with a parliamentary draftsman to prepare it. I could imagine that there was some intent on the part of the Home Office to expand our powers by putting this wording in. Or I could also imagine that the person who drafted it just didn't really think, and simply copied over the wording from the CHIS regulations. Then, well," she hesitated, "have you travelled much?"

"Yes, I travelled around Africa a bit as a student. Why?" replied Sally, a bit puzzled by the change of direction in the conversation.

"Well, I don't know if you've noticed around the world how in a lot of places there seem to be plenty of funds for putting up new buildings, while older ones go unmaintained."

Sally laughed. "Yes, I remember once I was in an old German hill station in Tanzania which was full of really solidly constructed buildings put up by the Germans which were now abandoned. And there was a team of European gap year volunteers who had gone out there to erect a new building, some sort of women's education centre. They could have refurbished one of the old buildings much more easily, and I'm sure it would have been of better quality than they could have built. But no, they wanted to construct a new building. Anyway, what's your point?"

"My point is that it's always more appealing to try to create something new than work with the old. If you work with the old then the time spent getting to grips with the old before you can go forward isn't visible to other people. If you just work on something new then you can look more productive. So if you're responsible for reviewing some legislation, it's more appealing to add to it, than spend time reviewing what is already there. And that's what I think happened here. The House of Lords proposed the addition of new provisions for the Act to protect minors, to require notification to a Judicial Commissioner, to ensure that criminal injuries compensation would still be payable to victims, and to spell out that certain acts which probably wouldn't be allowed anyway under the Human Rights Act would also not be allowed under CCAs. But it doesn't feel to me as if they really considered what needed to be changed in the existing draft. They just requested additions to it Of course I may be wrong. I would like to think that I am wrong. The Lords are all very learned, a lot of them are former judges, and it may well be that I'm missing something. But I have spent quite a lot of time looking at this legislation, and I can't see another explanation for why the grounds for authorising criminal acts are so widely drafted, when all they were supposed to be for was helping the CHIS to maintain his cover."

"Hmm, it's interesting, thank you."

"I mean, we can authorise crime if it's in the interests of the economic well-being of the country. Are trade unions in the interests of the economic well-being of the country? Arguably not. They negotiate pay-rises which have the effect of making British companies less profitable. So, as I read it, the legislation could allow us to authorise a CHIS to join a trade union, and to then authorise him to destroy the trade union's property, and access the union's bank account to expropriate all of its funds. All in the interests of the greater economic well-being of the UK. It's mind-boggling when you think about it."

They finished lunch, and Sally returned to her office. She called up Matt Elkins.

"Are you free next week?" she asked. "I've got a potential assignment for you."

"Yeah, what is it?"

"You know the Arctic, don't you? I need someone to go up to Sweden and follow a person of interest. All you need to do is shake this guy up a bit. Or maybe a lot." She laughed.

"OK. What's he doing up there?"

"Backpacking out in the wilderness somewhere. On his own. He's done it before. It strikes me as a bit dangerous, but anyway. Do you have any ideas what you can do to disturb him? I don't want you to injure him, but maybe you can scare him, make him uncomfortable."

"So he's camping then?"

"Yes"

"Hmm, maybe scare him at night. Or set his tent on fire. That would shake him up pretty badly."

"What would happen to him if he's inside the tent at the time?"

"He would probably live, but he might have really bad burns."

"That's too much. But if you could set it on fire when he's not in it, that could be good."

"OK, but why do you want to do this?"

"He's some sort of delusional character. Believe it or not he wants to claim asylum in Sweden. The powers-that-be at the Home Office don't like the idea at all. They're concerned that he has the potential to create public disorder. They want him shaken up while he's hiking so that hopefully he won't go ahead with it." Sally wasn't being quite honest about whose initiative this was.

"Good enough for me. I'm at your service. Will you get me a CCA for this?"

"Absolutely. Not a problem. Of course, it means you need to be a CHIS as well. We need to think about what kind of relationship you can enter into with him. I don't know if you could join him on his hike?"

"Well, I could, if he'll let me. But I'm not sure that will be the best way. Isn't intimidation more intimidating if the you don't know the person who's doing it to you? Maybe, I could just track him while he's up there, and set fire to his tent, etc?"

"Yes, but if you don't hike with him, then what kind of relationship have you got with him?"

"Maybe I could just have some sort of incidental relationship with him? Speak to him about the hike beforehand, or have a chat with him one night when he's camped somewhere?"

"OK, see what you can do in that regard. I'll give you access to his browsing history. Maybe that will give you the chance to contact him online and form a relationship that way? Otherwise perhaps you can establish what his movements in Sweden are going to be, and then you can accidentally bump into him somewhere and have a chat?"

"OK, good. I'll have to think about how much I need to charge for this, but I'll let you know."

"Fine. I'm sure we can reach an agreement on that."

Sally arranged for Matt to have access to Noel's browsing history as promised. She also got to work on drawing up the CHIS authorisation. The grounds for authorising it included the need for preventing disorder, which Sally felt was clearly made out here. They also included protecting public health. Noel's hike looked rather dangerous, thought Sally, it would be good for someone to keep an eye on him in case of an accident. So she added protecting public health in as an extra justification in the authorisation. She did not need anyone else's approval of the CHIS, so it was a fairly straightforward matter.

Sally could justify the criminal conduct authorisation on the ground that it was to prevent disorder. She wasn't totally comfortable about notifying the Judicial Commissioner about it; he might make queries at a higher level. So she decided that she would make the authorisation at the last minute just to minimise any potential problems. She could always wait the seven days that she was allowed, and claim that it had not been practical the notify the Commissioner earlier. There was bound to be some exceptional situation at work that she could point to justify it.

Matt spent some time looking over Noel's browsing history. He was interested to note Noel's interest in the story of the ghosts of Ähpár. If he could play on Noel's fears of these ghosts, that would be a great way to intimidate Noel. How to conjure them up, though?

The authorisations from Sally came through to Matt. The CHIS authorisation was complete, but the CCA was not signed or dated. Sally had explained in her cover note that he should let her know the day before he might need to commit any crime, and she would then sign this authorisation. That would then allow the maximum amount of time before the Judicial Commissioner had to be notified.

The evening after his discussion with Sally, Matt saw Noel, registering, and making an initial post on HikeBackCountry.com. In this post, he asked for information about the proposed hike. It was the perfect opportunity for Matt to contact him and form some sort of relationship. Matt immediately registered himself, and got into some lengthy discussions with Noel about the hike. He was now a CHIS, as required.  He was, of course, the real identity of Tromso2000.

Matt decided that he would need some assistants to play the ghosts. He had an acquaintance, Charles Routledge, who had a teenage son, Thomas, and he felt that they should be up to it. Matt phoned Charles, and he agreed to be involved, subject to receiving an appropriate fee. Matt called up Sally to put the full proposal to her. After a little discussion, a deal was struck. It included a bonus if Noel did not go on to claim asylum.

The House of Lords, in its review of the criminal conduct legislation, had succeeded in having a provision inserted to protect minors from suffering any injuries or psychological harm as a result of the operations in question. But this was easily circumvented, because it only applied where the CHIS was a minor. Although Thomas might be called on to commit criminal acts during the operation, (and be authorised to do so, because the acts were in connection with Matt's criminal conduct authorisation), Thomas himself was not a CHIS, so Sally did not need to be concerned with any harm that Thomas might come through his involvement in the mission.

Matt had been able to ascertain that Noel would be carrying a ReachMe device with him. That ought to be helpful in tracking Noel. It was quite common for the authorities to intercept communications from them. It was of course not public knowledge, but GCHQ was able to activate a facility on a ReachMe unit whereby it would transmit the user's location every five minutes as soon as the batteries were inserted. Users typically did this before the start of their hike, rather than have the potential added issue of having to find and install batteries in the case of an emergency. So this meant that GCHQ would be able to see Noel's location for the whole time he was in the mountains. If GCHQ was tracking a user's location then this was done without any concomitant display by the indicator lights on the unit, so the user was unaware that he was being tracked. The government had found this facility very useful in tipping off foreign authorities regarding a number of illegal encampments when hikers had taken a ReachMe for the purpose of a hike in to such a site. Matt contacted Stephen to set this up.

It was good that Matt had been able to establish a relationship with Noel online. This meant that there was no need to do so in Sweden. Matt, Charles and Thomas would now fly up to Tromsø, in northern Norway, where they would be collected by a former Norwegian military friend of Matt's by the name of Gunnar. Gunnar would drive them south and inland, before leaving them at a point where they could start walking, across the border, and for the best part of three days, to intercept Noel in Rapadalen. Matt had thought about simply hiring a car at the airport, and leaving it at the start point of the hike. But a hire car left for several days at the head of a remote valley might raise some questions. And he couldn't be certain that the hire car company wouldn't have a tracking device installed in the car, and become curious about just what it was that Matt was doing up in the mountains all that time. Of course he would say that he had gone hiking. But if news of Noel's coming ordeal became public, the hire car company might just put two and two together, and alert the police of its suspicions. So it was safer just to get Gunnar to drop the three of them off, and pick them up again once they returned.

## IX

## Wednesday 27<sup>th</sup> September

Matt had spent the previous night in a camouflaged bivvi bag, hidden under tree debris, up on Nammásj. He was now sitting comfortably perched on a grassy patch on the the top of Nammásj, equipped with high-powered binoculars. He was on his satellite phone to Stephen, back at GCHQ.

"Looks like he's finished lunch," said Matt, "He's stood up, and now he's throwing some antlers out into the lake."

"Whereabouts is he? Is he at your end of the boulder field?"

"Yeah, pretty much."

"That's the sacrificial site I think!" replied Stephen, with a laugh. "Sacrilege! Those antlers are holy. We can use that against him. Do you think that you will be able to keep following him as he gets closer?"

"Should be able to. The trees are relatively bare, and there's quite a big open area by the stream which he will have to cross. But once he gets close, I'll bed down. I'm well settled in up here. He'll never find me." Matt had instructions to track Noel during his hike, and do something to unsettle Noel that evening. Nothing so severe as to risk him returning to Aktse, perhaps just to throw a branch at his tent.

"I'll keep you informed. But I may not be able to see where he puts his tent up. Can you message me the exact co-ordinates once he's done so?" asked Matt.

"Sure, will do," replied Stephen.

*

## Morning of Thursday 28<sup>th</sup> September

Matt watched Noel from in the trees as he took down his tent and got ready for the day's hike. Once he had set off, Matt messaged Stephen to let him know of this. Stephen messaged him back:

"I will send you updates of his position throughout the day. Follow him, but don't come within less than half a mile of the last position I have given you. Once it looks like he has set up his tent, I will let you know exactly where that is. For now, just stay where you are. He's pretty slow, so you need to wait around a bit". Matt acknowledged the message. He then went to prepare himself some breakfast and pack up his belongings.

\*

## Evening of Thursday 28<sup>th</sup> September

Following Stephen's instructions, Matt had set up his bivouac on a ridge slightly beyond where Noel was, out of sight. His instructions were similar to those of the previous night, to try to unnerve Noel, but not do anything too extreme. Noel's campsite, on a ridge, was a bit of a problem for Matt, because he would have to be quite close to Noel's tent in order to disturb him. That meant that it would not be very easy for him to run off after disturbing Noel, without making some sound himself. He decided that he would wait until Noel was asleep and throw a rock up at his tent.

Matt watched from his ridge as Noel went out to clean his teeth. He watched as he went back into his tent, and waited for him to turn his torch off. He decided to wait a further hour. The Northern Lights started to show. Matt was impressed, although he had seen them many times before while training in Norway. The extra light was good. It meant that Matt could see his way over to Noel's tent quite easily without any need for a torch. When he felt that it was time, Matt quietly made his way over, carrying a rock that he had found for his mission, and began climbing the ridge towards Noel. As he did so, he heard a zip being undone. He froze. Noel was getting out of his tent. Matt lay down in the undergrowth, not far from Noel. What was he going to do if he was seen? Just run away, he decided. Even if Noel saw him that would still be quite unsettling. In the event, Noel did not see Matt but instead walked down into the meadow. Matt watched, and waited until Noel was clearly absorbed in watching the Northern Lights.

Matt realised that this was an opportunity to do something more creative. He slowly crawled towards the tent from where he caught sight of Noel down on the open area below the ridge. He spat on the zip, to lubricate it, so that it would make less noise as he opened it. Slowly, he unzipped it, and tied the flysheet back. He placed the rock that he had intended to throw, along with two others that he found nearby, in a symmetric arrangement, and crawled away, back down the ridge, and to where his bivouac was. This was getting to be quite fun. In the darkness he saw Noel walking around, calling out, and then packing up his tent and moving on. This was good. Matt's actions seemed to be having the sort of effect that he wanted.

*

## Friday 29<sup>th</sup> September

Stephen watched as Noel headed up the Rapadalen during the day, with Matt following behind him, at a distance.  Stephen was expecting Noel to continue through the pass behind Låddebákte and to camp somewhere beyond that. So he was surprised when he saw Noel heading off the path to the side. Noel then stopped, and after a while it started to look as if Noel was going to camp there for the night. Stephen messaged Matt to let him know this, and to tell him to head up to Skårkistugan and remain in the forest there. Stephen was aware that, at the altitude where Noel was, it was likely to snow that evening. If Matt were to try to disturb him, he would leave footprints and give himself away.

Charles and Thomas were in position, encamped in the trees just below the northwest side of the pass behind Låddebákte. These trees were just about at the limit of trees in the Rapadalen. Any further up the valley was above the treeline. Stephen called them up and told them to take no action that evening, but to await instructions the next day.

Matt decided that now was the time to get Sally to sign the criminal conduct authorisation, so he asked Stephen to arrange this. Charles's and Thomas's planned actions tomorrow in scaring Noel might would amount to assault if they put Noel in fear of violence. So the authorisation was now needed. Matt was the beneficiary of the authorisation, but Charles and Thomas were able to avail of it because the legislation covered criminal conduct carried out by or in relation to Matt, as the CHIS. The crimes themselves didn't have to be committed by Matt.

*

Saturday 30th September

Stephen watched as Noel set off in the morning and began climbing Låddebákte. Matt was able to confirm to him, having scanned with his binoculars, that Noel had left his tent in place, so it seemed fairly clear that Noel would be returning to it to spend a second night at the same location.

Stephen was very much hoping that he would be able to get Noel to turn back to Aktse. If he carried on, the terrain was rather open, so that it would be harder for Matt, Charles and Thomas to move about undetected. Also, Noel would have a number of different possible routes that he might take, and that would make planning harder for Stephen.

Matt spent the morning laying low in the forest. A later stage of the operation was going to entail the need to speak with a Scandinavian accent, so he was rehearsing this to himself. He had learnt quite good Norwegian in the course of military exercises in Norway, and so it came fairly naturally. He also wanted to review what he was and wasn't allowed to do under the criminal conduct authorisation. He had a copy of it with him, as well as a copy of the CHIS authorisation, so he spent a little time reading over these. He certainly planned to commit arson, and to steal some items from Noel, and that seemed fine. Assault was fine, and intimidation too, but he had to be sure not to commit more serious injury in the form of grievous bodily harm. He also had to stop short of torture, and that included mental torture. It sounded as if that would exclude a mock execution, and perhaps he would have to hold back a little on frightening Noel. But certainly there did seem to be quite a lot that he could do.

Once Stephen could see that Noel had started heading north on Låddebákte, so that Matt would not be visible from where he was, he called up Matt and asked him to do what he could to make the path to Skårkistugan unusable. If he could get Noel to come back down the mountain, he didn't want him going that way. If he went beyond Skårkistugan there was no path, and it would be hard to predict where he might go. Better that he go down the valley back towards Aktse. Matt obliged by spending much of the afternoon finding fallen trees in the forest and dragging them across the path.

Stephen instructed Charles and Thomas to wait at their campsite for further instructions. He had now received the signed criminal conduct authorisation from Sally, and informed Charles and Matt of this fact.

At around 3p.m. it became clear to Stephen from the location track from the ReachMe that Noel was heading back to his tent.

That was great news. It was unlikely that he would pack his tent up at this time of the day and move on somewhere else. He was going to sleep there again. Stephen called up Charles to tell him to be prepared to head up the pass come evening.

As evening fell, Stephen instructed Charles and Thomas to set off. As they approached the small lake behind Noel's campsite, they changed into their reindeer skin outfits, and left their other clothes under a rock. Quietly, they climbed the bluff above Noel's tent to wait for him to turn his torch off. Forty-five minutes later they climbed down to take up their positions outside Noel's tent. Charles found a good position where he could have his shadow fall over the tent, and stood there for a while. Clearing his throat a couple of times eventually seemed to disturb Noel. He heard Noel roll over in his tent. Charles continued waiting. He had time. Eventually he could hear that Noel was coming out of the tent, so he crept away, to crouch behind a rock, and allow Thomas to take over.

*

Once Charles and Thomas had succeeded in getting Noel to move on, Charles messaged the others to let them know that Noel was heading down. The plan now was to direct him further down the valley. Stephen kept Charles and Matt informed of Noel's position as he went, with a view to them following behind at a discreet distance. Thomas was getting cold so Charles stopped off at the gulley to set up a bivouac for him for the night, and once Noel had been successfully diverted down the valley from Skårkistugan, Matt started following him down.

Noel was slow, and Matt was frustrated that Charles had not shown up. He called him up.

"You coming?" he asked.

"Yeah, I'm on my way, sorry. I had to sort out Thomas. He was really cold. I made him something hot to drink and now he's alright. I'm on my way."

After some time, Stephen noticed that Noel had left the path. He messaged the others to let them know. Once it was clear that he had stopped, he told Matt to wait half an hour for further instructions; he was probably putting his tent up.

Once the half hour was up, Charles had still not reached Matt. Stephen messaged Matt.

"Go ahead and check to see if he's camping."

Matt very quietly approached Noel's location and saw his tent.

"Yes, he is. All quiet here. Shall I do it?"

"Yes, if you think he's asleep."

Matt laid down his rucksack, and got out a bottle that he had been carrying with him containing petrol. He prepared a thick bundle of sticks and grass which he soaked with petrol He collected several fist-size rocks and laid them down with the sticks by his rucksack. With utmost silence, he approached Noel's tent and poured the petrol over it. He retreated to his rucksack, put the sticks in the now empty bottle and began throwing the rocks at Noel's tent. As Noel got out, he lit the sticks, and threw the bottle, with the burning sticks, at the tent. He then ran off to be further away. He could see from a distance that the tent was burning well. He heard Noel scream in anger. Things were going to plan. His next step required him to be ahead of Noel, so he headed off, further down the valley.

## X

Feeling abjectly miserable, Noel got dressed. He still had a spare pair of socks, but his boots were wet through and those socks were not going to stay dry for long. It was miserable putting the boots on. He was going to be cold, that was clear. But better to keep walking and generate some body heat than sit there shivering and getting ever colder. His only concern now was to get out, so he packed all of his clothes and his sleeping bag but left behind much of his food and his blackened tent poles to keep down the weight he would have to carry. He took a photo of what was left of his tent, for the record, and set off.

Noel headed back to the path. He just wanted the night to be over, and to be back at Aktse as soon as possible, regaining some heat in his body. The horrible wet snow was still falling. He was really cold, and shivering. He reached the big stream close to the ridge where he had camped. He was too cold to sit down and remove his boots, so again he just marched right through. He was full of hatred for whomever had done this to him.

Every step was unpleasant. Slowly, Noel started to round Lulep Spádnek, where he had stopped for lunch by the river a few days earlier. In the dark, it had all the presence of a mountain, even though really of course it was quite small. He reached an open area in the path which he recognised. It was where he had had lunch on the way up above the river. He continued on, back into the forest. Soon he arrived at the second, smaller of the two clearings. Suddenly, as he entered the clearing, he was dazzled by a bright white torch, being shone straight in his eyes. It temporarily blinded him. Somebody was there, but he couldn't see them. He cried out in protest.

"I've got a knife," came a voice, in what Noel took to be a Swedish accent. "Just stay calm and don't do anything stupid." Noel could just about see the glint of a knife close to his neck. "Drop your walking poles."

"What do you want?"

"Just do as I tell you. Drop your walking poles," repeated the voice. Noel felt a jab from the knife in his chest. He dropped his poles. He was standing close to the steep drop down to the river, his back to it. He could hear the sound of the water rushing below.

"Now, give me your headtorch."

"What are you going to do?"

"JUST GIVE ME YOUR HEADTORCH," screamed the voice. Noel did so. The source of the voice took it and put it in his pocket. Noel could see it still shining through.

"Now you are going to slowly take off your boots, tie them together at the laces, and give them to me."

"What? I'm going to die here if you leave me like this."

"Just do it. I know you have some sandals with you. Sit down and take your boots off."

"Please don't do this." Noel sat down with his rucksack still on and removed his boots before handing them over. There was no question of running away. He was tired, had a steep drop behind him down to the river, and now no headtorch.

"Now you are going to give me your phone and your camera."

"I don't know who you are, or what you want, but you're not going to get away with this."

"Just do as I say and I promise I won't hurt you."

Noel got his phone out from the pocket of his jacket, and his camera out from his rucksack.

"You'll pay for this," said Noel as he handed the items over.

"Thank you. Sit down again." Noel did as he was instructed.

"Now tell me why you are here."

"I've been hiking, that's all."

"In the middle of a night such as this?"

"Yes. No, tell you what, I'm a lunatic, that's why." Noel didn't care what the assailant thought of him and thought that maybe he could throw him off-balance with an unexpected reply.

"You are indeed. Where are you going tonight?"

"I want to go to Aktse."

"I see. You are very strange. And where will you go after that?"

"Away from here. Away from people who set my tent on fire and set on me in the middle of the night."

"I'm sorry to hear if your tent has been burnt. But it's a good idea that you go away. Where are you from?"

"England."

"So you will go straight back there?"

"Yes. I'm flying back in a few days."

"LIAR. You are going to Örebro. Why are you lying to me?"

How the hell did this man know that? Noel was starting to lose his will to resist.

"How can you possibly know that?"

"Never mind. I will ask the questions. Why are you going to Örebro?"

"Just to visit a friend who lives there."

"And what's their name?"

"Jens," Noel extemporised.

"Jens who?"

"Wiedermann." Noel couldn't think of a Swedish surname fast enough, and what he came up with was unfortunately rather more German.

"YOU ARE LYING TO ME AGAIN," screamed the voice, with another jab of the knife, "Tell me the real reason now, Noel".

It was deeply disturbing to Noel to realise that the man knew his name. He was on the verge of tears.

"How do you know my name?"

"I know everything. Tell me why you are going to Örebro."

"Why are you asking me, if you already know everything?"

"I want to hear it from you. Tell me, Noel."

"Just a silly idea."

"WHAT SILLY IDEA?"

"Nothing"

"TELL ME" screamed the voice.

"I was going to claim asylum there."

"YOU WERE GOING TO CLAIM ASYLUM?"

"Yes, I'm persecuted in England. I felt that Sweden would help me."

"PERSECUTED? IN ENGLAND. We have people come here from Syria because they have had a bomb land on their house and half their family killed. What kind of persecution do you have in England?"

"I'm discriminated against because I'm white and male and heterosexual. I have no life there."

"YOU ARE DISCRIMINATED AGAINST BECAUSE YOU ARE WHITE AND MALE AND HETEROSEXUAL! What kind of nonsense is this? I have never heard anything so ridiculous in my whole life. You are not persecuted. You have no life because of your own decisions. Coming here hiking in the mountains on your own, and then thinking that we will listen to your story here. What kind of crazy man are you?"

Noel broke down. He couldn't take this any more.

"Crying won't help you. Just tell me that you're not going to claim asylum, and are going to go straight back to England after this."

"Whatever you want."

"NO, TELL ME WHAT I SAID."

"I'm not going to claim asylum, and I'm going back to England after this."

"TELL ME AGAIN, LOUDER."

"I'M NOT GOING TO CLAIM ASYLUM, AND I'M GOING TO GO BACK TO ENGLAND AFTER THIS."

"Swear to me that that is what you are going to do."

"I SWEAR TO YOU THAT I AM NOT GOING TO CLAIM ASYLUM AND AM GOING TO GO BACK TO ENGLAND."

"Good, that is what I wanted to hear. I think you had taken leave of your senses. But it is good that you see some sense now. And Noel," the assailant dropped the tone of his voice, "when you get back to England, please get some help. There are people there who will help you. But you do not belong in this country, and never will do. Adjö."

The assailant walked off into the forest, with Noel's headtorch, boots, camera and phone, and headed up the valley, leaving Noel, distraught. The assailant was of course Matt. He had learnt how to say goodbye in Swedish for a small final flourish. He soon reached the second, larger clearing, from where he called up Stephen and gave him a rundown of his interrogation. He agreed that Stephen could now go home and get some sleep.

Matt, Charles and Thomas would now hike back across the border to where Gunnar would collect them again. Ending the operation there meant that they should be able to avoid the Swedish authorities who might potentially start looking for Noel's assailants. It was very remote country across to Norway, and they were unlikely to be apprehended. The Swedes would have no idea which way they had gone, and there was so much country to search. It would take them two days to reach the border, and then another half a day to reach the pickup point. They would hike mostly at night, bedding down among trees and in any caves that they could find to avoid detection. It was in order to give themselves time before Noel alerted the authorities that Matt had taken Noel's boots and headtorch. Unable to see in the dark, Noel would have to wait where he was until dawn. That, combined with only having his sandals to walk in, meant that it would probably take him all of the next day to walk to Aktse, if that was what he chose to do. If he stayed put, then Stephen would have to forward the S.O.S. alert some time the next afternoon. Noel couldn't be made to wait there for two nights; the risk of hypothermia was too great. Imposing that on him would seem to amount to torture, which of course was not allowed. Noel would protest to the Swedish authorities that he had set the alarm off some 16 hours before the helicopter arrived. But Outdoor Tracking Services would be unable to explain the discrepancy, and there would be little further to be done about it.

Before hiking out, Matt had a few things to do that might help cast doubt on any version of events that Noel would give to the authorities. In relation to Noel's boots, he would tie them together by the laces and catch them on a branch in the stream, just below the crossing. When Noel claimed that his boots had been stolen, and they were later found at the stream crossing, it would look more as if he had simply dropped them while crossing the stream. Matt would also return to the site of the tent fire, and collect the petrol bottle. If it could look as if Noel had simply had a tent fire due to his own inattention, that would be very helpful.

Matt had some cause to hope that he had intimidated Noel sufficiently such that he would not claim asylum. He would be giving the Swedish authorities quite a bit of trouble in either having to be rescued, or showing up at Aktse in a terrible state. He would then be giving an unsubstantiated story about how he had been set on in the mountains by people in reindeer skin outfits, and that someone had set his tent on fire. His story would seem hard to believe. For him to add on top of all that that he wished to claim asylum would really make the Swedes' eyes roll. He would seem like a fantasist. Of course there was the possibility that Matt's actions might just make Noel more resolute. But Matt then would still get paid, he just wouldn't receive his bonus. Time would tell.

## XI

As Matt stood in the clearing, a slight movement from the other side of the river caught his eye in the darkness. He shone his torch across. There were two people. It looked to be Charles and Thomas. So they had both come down after all, and finally got there. He was irritated that it had taken them so long, and also that they had somehow managed to end up on the wrong side of the river. What on earth had they been doing? He waved at them and shouted, but the sound from the river was too much, and they were clearly never going to hear. They didn't wave back though either. So Matt called Charles up on his satellite phone.

"Charles, it's Matt."

"Sorry I'm on my way. It's just hard following this damn path in the dark," said Charles.

"What do you mean? I can see you both from here. Why are you on the wrong side of the river?"

"Don't know what you're talking about, mate. Thomas is back in his bivvy bag. And I'm somewhere in the middle of this damn forest."

"Ha ha! I can see you both across the river. Standing right opposite me."

"I swear to you, we are not there."

"Well, who the hell am I looking at then?"

"I don't know. We are not there."

"This had better not be a joke."

Matt froze. Who on earth was it over there if it wasn't Charles and Thomas? As well as being visible from where Matt now was, they would also have had a clear line of sight to where he had interrogated Noel, just downriver. They must have been watching. Who on earth was it? This was unbelievable. How could there be anyone else out here in the middle of this cold wet night? He was still on the phone to Charles.

"Well I swear to you, there are two people on the other side of the river, watching me. I don't know who the hell they are. They're just standing there, and they're giving me the creeps. They must have seen everything I just did. We're going to have to get out of here quick."

"Shit."

Matt continued watching. In horror and disbelief, he observed the two figures as they slowly rose up, and floated out to a point above the river. More dark figures appeared on the water, both upstream and downstream. They too began floating in silence across the water towards him. The illegitimate child and demons of Ähpár had awoken. In expropriating their image, and committing such acts of aggression against Noel, Matt had broken the natural order of Rapadalen. The wrath of the spirits would be immense. Do child ghosts and mountain demons respect criminal conduct authorisations? Not very likely. Had Sally thought about that problem? No. Matt was about to get his comeuppance.

## XII

## Sunday, 1st October

Noel closed his eyes and took in some deep breaths. He was of
course relieved that his assailant seemed to have finished with
him. Now he had to figure out his next steps, but he wanted a few
moments to try to blot the situation out of his head. He opened
his eyes, and looked around. He couldn't see much in the dark,
but could make out the basic features of the clearing and the long
drop down towards the river, the sound of which he could hear.
He picked up his rucksack and walked across in his socks to the
side of the clearing away from the river, and continued a few
metres into the trees. He needed the shelter, and preferred to be
hidden in case his assailant returned.

Once in the cover of the trees, Noel sat down on a fallen tree, and
fumbled around in his rucksack for his sandals, which he put on
together with his remaining dry clothes, and his waterproofs back
on top. There was no way that he could go anywhere before it
was light, so he decided that he in fact didn't need his sandals,
and instead he just put feet into a plastic bag to keep them warm
and dry. He sat with his rucksack in front of him, his head resting
upon it. He was going to listen out for a rescue helicopter,
although he doubted that the rescue services would fly in the
dark. He was shell-shocked, but grateful to be unhurt, and
hopeful that his ordeal would soon be over.

His mind turned to how it could be that his assailants had seemed
to be able to find him wherever he went. Did that fact mean that
they knew where he was sitting right now? It was an
uncomfortable realisation that he might now be being watched,
or that his assailant might return at any moment. The fact that
the two people had found him on Låddebákte was not so hard to
explain. Although his tent was a dull green colour and he had
camped away from the path, someone scanning with binoculars

from the valley would have been able to see it fairly easily. Although of course they still had to be taking quite an interest in him to go to the trouble. But in the forest that night? He had got there well after dark, and had camped some distance into the trees, so surely it would have been very hard for someone to have found him. If someone had been following him, he would have noticed them.

It all suggested that somehow he was being tracked by means an electronic device. He no longer had his phone. But if there was no phone reception here in the mountains, was there really any way that someone could have tracked him by means of his phone? The phone had a GPS receiver. But surely that wouldn't emit information about his location. So it seemed unlikely anyone could have tracked him via the phone. Could it be the ReachMe? He got it out and looked at it. It was still flashing orange to indicate that he had triggered the alarm, and that it was broadcasting his position. He had only turned it on after his tent was set alight though. Could it have actually been broadcasting his position before he turned it on? Presumably it was technologically feasible for it to do so. But would it really be set up like that? What an utter betrayal of trust if the object that you are bringing with you for your safety is actually giving you away, and doing so to some unknown, malign authority? He looked at it with a sense of extreme unease. Was it a friend, or was it a foe?

Noel concluded that he still had to give the ReachMe the chance to get him rescued. For now though, he would take the batteries out, and move a few hundred metres to a different location. If someone had been tracking him then they would no longer be able to do so. It wasn't very pleasant, struggling through the trees in the dark, and probably he didn't manage to travel quite a far as he thought he had, but before long he had found a spot to sit down again and pass the rest of the night.

Naturally, Noel didn't sleep. He was too uncomfortable and too cold. But over the course of the night he fell into and out of a state of drowsiness, his head resting on his rucksack. He also kept half an ear out for any sounds that might indicate his assailant was approaching once more. Eventually he looked up, and was pleased to see a slight lightening of the sky. The sleet and snow had stopped. He dozed a bit more, and there was then a reasonable amount of light around. Although he felt groggy, he felt a lot of relief to have made it through the night, and be seeing the dawn. He looked around the location where he had chosen to spend the night. He had some rocks behind him, but in front of him were just trees. He couldn't see the path, although he could hear the sound of the river in the distance. The path could not be far away.

As Noel looked around, he could see that it appeared that someone clearly had been where he was before, for there appeared to be some papers wedged up in a tree in in front of him, at the base of a branch. It can be surprising what traces of humanity you find deep in a forest, when you might think that no-one had any business to ever go there. Sometimes scientific researchers have tagged trees with bits of tape to carry out surveys, and left these tags behind. Occasionally you might even come across a camera trap, set up to see what wildlife is passing by. Perhaps these papers were to do with some such research, and someone had left them behind. In any case, Noel decided that it was time to stretch his legs, so he put his sandals on and got up to have a look at the object in the tree. He picked it out. It was a plastic document wallet, with the papers inside.

Noel sat down with the documents. There were just two sheets of paper, folded in half together. On the outside of them, someone had written, in the most beautiful handwriting, in black ink, the words "Geahčastala kaleanddar njeallje bahá rihkus láhkadieđalaš

2007". He didn't imagine that it would be very interesting, but he unfolded the papers anyway. And his jaw dropped.

The two documents were both on headed paper that he recognised immediately. It was that of his employer, UK Visas and Immigration. They were both in the form of letters, addressed to a certain Matt Elkins. The first letter was headed "Covert Human Intelligence Source Authorisation". He was appalled to see that It instructed Matt Elkins to enter into a covert relationship with him in order to obtain information about his intentions in Sweden. It stated that his actions had the potential to foment disorder in the United Kingdom, and that the author of the letter considered the formation of a covert relationship to be necessary to prevent such disorder. The author was his boss, Sally Krosen. So it seemed she had sent someone to spy on him while he was hiking, and he had accidentally left the authorisation in the forest. He was aghast. The second letter was headed "Criminal Conduct Authorisation". It too was signed by Sally Krosen, and it authorised this Matt Elkins to commit certain listed crimes against him. So this was what had been going on! What an utter betrayal. But what power he now had to have these documents in his possession.

How had this Matt Elkins formed a relationship with him, Noel wondered. Had he met him somewhere? On the train perhaps? Or could he be the man at the hut at Aktse? Was the short conversation he had had with him enough to constitute a relationship? Maybe. It did after all seem a bit surprising that the man was there after the huts were supposed to be closed. Had he been planted there for the purpose of this mission? Things started to add up in Noel's head. The man was Swedish, surely, as seemingly was the man who had mugged him the night before. That added up. But then who was Matt Elkins, with such an English name?

What of the handwritten note on the reverse of the authorisations? Noel guessed that this must have been written by his assailant, but it seemed to be in Swedish. So presumably Matt Elkins was just a pseudonym, and there was no English person involved. The assailant had had a Swedish accent, after all. He carefully put the documents in his rucksack. He then decided that he needed to warm himself up, so he began jumping up and down to get his circulation going again.

But how did the documents end up in the tree? As it turns out, the demons of Ähpár are not purely malevolent. They had found the documents in the inside pocket of Matt's jacket, and removed them. After a bit of research, they had established the importance of the documents to Noel's situation, and had deposited them in front of him overnight, together with the handwritten note, for him to find in the morning. They wanted to help Noel.

A distant throbbing sound from the direction of Aktse caught Noel's attention. A helicopter! Excellent, someone was coming to rescue him. But he had removed the batteries from his ReachMe and was now some distance from where his location would have last been broadcast. He grabbed his rucksack and rushed out to the path. As he got there, he saw the helicopter, level with him in the valley. He jumped up and down and waved, but there wasn't much chance of the pilot seeing him through the trees. The helicopter carried on up the valley. He was frustrated to see it continue, clearly well past the point where he had triggered the alarm the night before. Why was it going so far?

Noel stopped, and reinserted the batteries in his ReachMe. The lights started flashing as expected. He headed on up to the clearing, hoping that the helicopter would soon return. The helicopter was small, and he was confident that there was room for it to land in the clearing should it come back. He got out a granola bar to eat, and started waiting.

Noel did feel rather uncomfortable waiting at the site of the previous night's interrogation, and was worried that his assailant would reappear. But he didn't think that there would be another suitable clearing for some distance if he walked down the valley, so he decided to wait where he was. Nonetheless he kept looking over his shoulder uneasily to see if anyone was there.

Noel was started to ask himself whether he should start walking out when, after about an hour, he heard the sound of the helicopter again. He soon saw it, coming towards him down the valley. He waved with both arms to indicate that he was in trouble and needed help. This time he was sure he must be seen. So he was crestfallen when, again, the helicopter went right past him. What was going on? Could the pilot not tell where he was from the ReachMe?

Then, to Noel's great relief, the helicopter made a turn, and started approaching him. He put his rucksack on, and stood well back, as the helicopter landed in the clearing. The pilot slowed the rotors, and lent over to open the door.

"Are you OK?" he shouted.

"NO," shouted Noel back.

"OK, come in, I take you," shouted the man, gesturing to Noel to get in.

Noel climbed inside. There were just two seats in the helicopter, and Noel was seated beside the pilot. The pilot gave him some ear protectors to wear, and quickly took off again. Noel He looked down at the Ráhpaädno delta below him as he flew back to Aktse. Within a few minutes they had landed. Was the man who looked after the cabins going to be here?

As the rotor blades slowed, the pilot removed his ear defenders and pointed at Noel's feet.

"You were hiking in those?" he asked, noting Noel's sandals. The man spoke with a strong accent. He was well built, with features that looked to be quite well chiselled by the weather.

"Somebody stole my boots," replied Noel.

"They stole your boots? I have never heard of that before. From your tent I suppose?"

"No, they mugged me."

"They mugged you?" replied the man, incredulously.

"Yes, with a knife."

"With a knife! So now they have two pairs of boots I suppose. Not very useful."

"I know. It's a long story."

"I have to go back to my house," said the man, "But I think you should go speak to Andreas in the cabins, tell him about your stolen boots."

"Andreas is the person who look after the cabins, is he?"

"Yes."

"Maybe I met him before. Is he definitely here now, do you know?"

"Yes, he should be. I spoke to him this morning before I set off."

If Andreas was the person who had terrorised Noel last night, he would have to have done a pretty good job in walking back. But it was possible.

"OK, I will. Thank you so much for rescuing me. But can I ask a question?"

"Yes"

"Why did you go right past me, and only come back after an hour? You knew where I was didn't you?"

"No, I didn't know you were there. I went up to herd my reindeer. I saw you waving when I came back, so turned around." The man was a Sami reindeer herder. Sami frequently use helicopters nowadays to herd their reindeer. It is much easier than doing so on foot. The man wanted to herd his reindeer down the Rapadalen towards Aktse, where some of them would be slaughtered for meat. The remainder of the herd would later continue to the lowland forests to the east, to spend the winter.

"I requested a rescue with my tracking device," said Noel. "If you weren't the rescue helicopter then maybe there is another one coming. I think we need to let the authorities know."

"I understand. I will speak to them."

The pilot got on his radio and had a conversation in Swedish with someone. He asked Noel for his name. After getting off the radio he told Noel that he had spoken to the police, who said they had not received any request for a rescue. Noel looked concerned. The man continued and said that the police had now been informed that he had been rescued, so that if a request came in, they would know he had already been rescued. But now he must go and speak to Andreas. Noel got out from the helicopter, thanked the pilot again, and went up to the cabins to find Andreas. He was apprehensive that he might be about to meet his tormentor again. But it had to be done.

Noel could see no sign of activity at the cabins, so he knocked on the door of what seemed to be the main building. There was no answer, so he called out. A man came out from behind an equipment shed. It was the man Noel had spoken to when he passed through Aktse at the start of his hike. He didn't look as if he had been up all night.

"Oh, you are back again. You didn't go to Suorva?" asked the man, glancing at Noel's inadequate footwear.

"No, there were people who didn't want me to."

"People who didn't want you to?"

"Yes, like burning my tent, and threatening me with a knife."

The man gave Noel a puzzled look. "Come now. This is a national park where people come just for some hiking. It's not a war zone. Who would do such a thing?"

"I know. But I'm telling you it happened. And I have some documents that explain it."

"Well, if you insist it happened, then you must tell the police."

"Yes, I want to tell the police. I have no phone. Do you have a radio or something I can use to speak to them?"

"Yes, come inside, we have a radio you can use."

"Thanks. Are you Andreas?"

"Yes"

"Can I ask you a question? Have you been here the whole time since I was last here?"

"Yes, apart from I went down to the lake. But yes, I have been here."

"Did you see anyone else heading up the valley?"

"No, no-one apart from you."

Perhaps Andreas wasn't the tormentor. He seemed too agreeable for one thing, his voice didn't seem quite the same, and he certainly didn't give the impression of having been up all night walking back to Aktse from the site where Noel had been mugged. Andreas led Noel inside the main hut and offered him a seat. He had a radio set there on which he dialled someone up, and spoke to them for a short while in Swedish before handing over to Noel.

"OK, this is Police Inspector Kristina Lindberg. She is in Gällivare. Please tell her what happened."

Noel proceeded to give an account of everything that had happened, right from the disturbance on Nammásj, through to the events of the previous night. He got to the point where Matt had interrogated him about claiming asylum in Sweden, and thought it better to gloss over that. He could tell that Kristina was having some trouble believing his account. Andreas also looked a bit disbelieving. So Noel left out any mention of claiming asylum. He didn't want make the situation sound even more extraordinary than it already did.

"But why would somebody want to do all of this?" asked Kristina, "Just for fun? I can't imagine how much work it must be to do all that."

Noel got up and reached into his rucksack. He pulled out the two authorisation documents that he had found in the tree at dawn. He placed them down in front of Andreas and explained what he understood about how the operation against him had been planned on the basis of preventing disorder in the UK.

"And what disorder were you planning? Were you going to do it in the mountains?" asked Andreas, incredulously.

"I wasn't planning any disorder. But I had an idea, it was probably a crazy one. I wanted to come to Sweden to claim asylum."

Andreas looked up at him in surprise. Noel continued "The government would have been worried that if I did that, it would look bad on them, a British person claiming asylum in Sweden, and would lead to protests in England."

"So how do you have these documents? Does your government give people against whom it wants to commit these acts copies of the documents?"

"No, or course they don't. But, OK, maybe you won't believe this either, but I found them wedged in a tree this morning. I think that the people who were victimising me must have left them there by mistake."

Andreas exhaled sharply. It was obvious that what Noel was saying was too much to believe.

"What do you want to do, Kristina?" he asked.

"I think it is best that he comes to Gällivare, and speaks to us. Can he get to Saltoluokta and then take the bus here in the afternoon?"

"OK, I'll see if we can get him a helicopter ride, and I'll let you know," turning to Noel, Andreas continued "Let's go and speak to Erland, who flew you here just now, and see if he's OK to fly you to Saltoluokta this afternoon."

After lunch Erland transferred Noel by helicopter to Saltoluokta. Saltoluokta lies down-valley from Suorva, Noel's original intended destination. There is another collection of cabins at Saltoluokta, with accommodation. It lies south of a large lake, with the road to Gällivare on the opposite side. Normally there would be a boat service across the lake, and Erland could have dropped Noel at Saltoluokta to take that, before getting the bus on the other side of the lake. But the main season in the mountains had now ended, and the boat was not operating. So Erland dropped Noel

119

on the north side of the lake, close to the road. Noel was then able to catch the afternoon bus to Gällivare. Once on it, he looked out of the bus window. He was leaving the mountains and his hike was well and truly over. Outside it was raining quite hard, and from the comfort of the bus, the outdoors that he had come to experience now looked very uninviting. On arriving at Gällivare, he was met by Kristina, who took him to the police station to give a full account. Kristina asked him where he worked.

"At UK Visas and Immigration, in the south of London."

"So the same place as this lady, Sally Krosen, then?"

"She is my boss."

"Oh OK. How is your relationship with her?"

"She's not a very easy woman to work for."

"So it would be fair to say that you don't really get on very well with her?"

"That is true," he said "but I never could have imagined that she would do something like this to me".

"Hmm," said Kristina. "OK, I would like to take copies of these documents if you don't mind, if you can just wait here."

Kristina got up, and left the room, to find a photocopier. Noel wasn't feeling as good as he had hoped he would in getting his story across to the police. From their point of view it must look as if he was just making the whole thing up. It was such an extraordinary story after all. He could easily have produced the documents himself.

After about twenty minutes, Kristina returned. Either there had been a long queue for the photocopier, or she had been talking to someone else while out of the room.

"Look, I know my story must seem hard to believe," said Noel.

"Well, we're not making any decisions just yet," replied Kristina.

"I find it hard to believe. But I raised it with the man at Aktse, and well, here I am. All I can do is tell the truth."

"I understand. I spoke to one of my colleagues, and we feel that the best thing is if you can stay in Gällivare tonight, and we speak again tomorrow. I know that you didn't sleep last night, so it is best that you go and get some rest, and maybe think things over. Do you have somewhere to stay?"

"No, I wasn't expecting to be back yet."

"OK, we can help you find somewhere, don't worry."

Kristina handed the two documents back to Noel. "I have one question still. What do you understand by this wording on the back of this letter?" She pointed to the handwritten note that Noel had first seen.

"I have no idea. I was hoping you might be able to tell me what it means."

"No, I can't read it. It's Sami, not Swedish. It's very strange that it's written there. I've taken a copy of it, and we will find out what it means."

"Good, I will be interested to know. Thank you."

Kristina drove Noel to a hotel in town. "Get a good night's sleep. We will call you in the morning. And if you feel that there is anything that you would like to revise in your account tomorrow, that is fine. We will understand. It is clear that you have had some difficult experiences, so it may be better to tell us your story once you've had a rest."

*

121

After sleeping through much of the day, Charles and Thomas got up and prepared something to eat. They were going to walk through the night, from their hideout in the trees, as far towards Norway as they could. If Matt had been intercepted, as seemed to be the case, there was a good chance the Swedish authorities would now be on the lookout for them, so they needed to travel as fast as they could. But there was a problem. Matt, in his plan, had envisaged the three of them walking across fairly dry tundra all the way out to Norway. But he had little experience of the area in autumn. He hadn't thought about the fact that the tundra might be covered in snow at this time of year. During the afternoon, while it had been raining where Noel was in the bus, here it had snowed, and there was now about two inches of snow lying on the ground. It had now stopped snowing. Charles and Thomas's route would take them higher, across quite an open plateau, where there would only be more snow. Their tracks would be easy to follow for anyone who found them and was inclined to do so.

As it started to get dark, Charles and Thomas set off. It was hard work in the snow, although the moon, and for a while the Northern Lights, meant that they were able to find their way without headtorches. Their route took them up the narrow Sarvesvágge valley before crossing out of the Sarek National Park into the adjacent Padjelanta National Park. This park is of a similar size to Sarek, but the terrain is flatter. It extends all the way to the Norwegian border. There are a few small Sami settlements on the edges of two very large natural lakes, Virihaure and Vastenjaure, so there was a possibility that other people might be around.

Charles and Thomas struggled on through the night, across the tundra. As it started to get light they were still about ten miles from the Norwegian border. Given that there were likely to be a few reindeer herders around during the day who might notice them they decided to stop and rest up, before carrying on into Norway the next night. They found a suitably sheltered location amongst some large boulders, and made a rudimentary camp there. They were very tired. Hopefully their tracks in the snow would be covered by further snow falling, or snow being blown by the wind, so that no-one would be able to locate them.

## XIII

## Monday 2nd October

Noel slept soundly, and got up just in time to make the last serving of breakfast in his hotel. While he was eating, a receptionist came up to him and asked him to take a phone call. It was from Kristina Lindberg.

"We would like to ask you some more questions," she said, "can you be ready to come into the police station if we pick you up in, say, half an hour?"

Noel felt a dread about the prospect of having to justify his story further. He would have preferred to be being told that the police had made some arrests than that they wanted to question him. "OK" he said, "I'll be at reception if you want to pick me up."

Kristina collected Noel up and drove him to the police station. She said very little while in the car. She took him into an interview room. She went straight to the point.

"I have to tell you that we have found a body," she said.

"What? Where? Who?" Noel had not been expecting to hear that.

"Before you say anything further, I have to tell you that you are under suspicion in relation to this. There is no easy way to say it, but you are under suspicion of assault, and manslaughter or murder." Noel could hardly bear to hear the words being spoken. Did everyone have it in for him on this trip? He had thought that he had got over his ordeal. He had been victimised and now he was a suspect. His instinct was to protest his innocence, but Kristina continued:

"You have the right to a lawyer, if you wish. And you do not have to say anything. You will also have a right in due course to see the evidence that we obtain. Do you wish to have a lawyer present?"

"Fine. If you're accusing me of something as serious as that, I'd better have a lawyer present."

"We are not accusing you. We just have suspicions which we cannot avoid. There is a difference. I will get a lawyer for you. Please wait."

Kristina left the room and returned a few minutes later, with the duty lawyer, who introduced himself to Noel, and sat down.

"I would like you to run through again what happened when you say you were held at knifepoint by the river, please." Noel obliged. The lawyer looked astonished as he heard the history.

"Did you try to fight back at all?" Katrina asked.

"No, it would have been useless. The man had a big knife, and a headtorch which he kept shining right in my eyes, so I couldn't even see properly. I wouldn't have stood a chance."

"And what happened at the end of the interaction? Did he run off?"

"No, I think he just walked off, so far as I recall."

"Did you go after him?"

"No, remember he had a knife, and I had no boots to wear, only my sandals. What use would it have been to have done that?"

"Did you see him again at all after that?"

"No, not at all. I saw no-one until I was picked up by the helicopter."

"Where did you go after he left you?"

"As I told you, I just went into the forest and down the valley a bit. I didn't want to be found."

"Did you stay there all night?"

"Well, I moved at one point because I was concerned that I was being tracked through my emergency device. But I stayed in the forest."

"Did you go out into the riverbed at any time?"

"No, I didn't."

"Can you tell me again how you found the documents you showed me yesterday?"

"As I said, I just found them in a tree. Why?"

"Because it all seems a bit convenient. You just happened to stop by a tree where Mr. Elkins just happened to have accidentally left the documents. Don't you think?"

"Oh, I see what you mean. Well, it is what happened."

"Did you bring the documents with you from England?"

"No. I had never heard of this Matt Elkins before I found the documents in the tree."

"One explanation would be that you went after him after he mugged you, beat him up, or even killed him, and took the documents off him then."

"So the body that you found is his."

"It is, yes. But can you please address what I said."

"It would make no sense. As I said, it would have been impossible for me to take him on. And if I had, I would have been more concerned about getting my boots back than wondering if he had any interesting documents on him."

Katrina was silent for a while. Eventually she said "I think it would be helpful if you can come with us to Rapadalen today, to take us where you say these things happened. We would also like to see your tent, and perhaps you can help us find it. Can you do that?"

"Yes, I will do whatever is necessary to help you get to the bottom of this. I don't have any proper shoes to wear though."

"We will find you some boots. What size do you take?"

"Er, nine, English size."

"OK, we'll sort it out. If you can wait here please."

Katrina returned with some Swedish police boots, continental size 43, and asked Noel to try them on. She had also procured some sunglasses and a coat for Noel, explaining that there was quite a bit of snow on the ground in the valley.

"Can you tell me how the body was found?" asked Noel.

"Yes, Erland, the man who picked you up by helicopter yesterday, was out again today, and he saw the body lying on a sandbank in the river. He called us up to let us know, and we have already sent two officers out there to investigate."

"And you know for a fact that the body is that of Matt Elkins?"

"Yes, we found his passport on him." So clearly the name was not a pseudonym, as Noel had thought.

"Well, if he's the person who attacked me, I can tell you he does a good Swedish accent."

The boots were a good fit, and Katrina drove Noel out to the local helicopter base for the flight back to Rapadalen. He couldn't stop thinking over the fact that it seemed his assailant had died. All he had done was walked away from him. There didn't seem any reason for it to have happened.

It was a beautiful sunny day. Noel would have found the helicopter flight exhilarating were his status as a murder suspect not weighing so heavily on his mind. As the mountains got closer, the ground below began to have a covering of snow. The flight took about 45 minutes. As they approached the landing site, close to where Noel had camped on the ridge on his third night, Noel saw some signs of police activity out in the river, presumably examining the site where Matt had been found. The helicopter turned and landed in the clearing close to the ridge. There was already another helicopter there on the ground, presumably the one that had transported the police who were already on site. An officer was waiting for them there. As they got out of the helicopter, he beckoned them over.

"Allow me to introduce myself. I am Inspector Lars Olsson. I presume you must be Noel. Thank you for coming out here today."

"It's fine. I just want to prove to you that I had no part in the death of this man," replied Noel.

"Of course. We have found some items, and would like you to identify them for us please." He opened the helicopter door and showed Noel some boots, walking poles, a headtorch, camera and phone. Noel of course immediately recognised them as his.

"Where did you find them?" asked Noel.

"Just by the river, a little way down from here. Do you recognise them?"

"Yes, they are mine."

"All of the items?"

"Yes."

"I can't let you have them back just yet. We need to do some tests. But we would like you to take us to some of the locations where you say you were attacked. And I understand you have some photos of the stones which were left outside your tent, and of your burnt tent. Are they on your phone or your camera?"

"On my camera."

"OK, we'll try to go to each of those locations, and I'll bring the camera. You can show us the photos. I would be interested to see the stones if they are still there, and the remains of your tent."

Noel, Katrina and Lars commenced a tour of the nearby sites where Noel had been harassed. They began by going downstream.

The three of them reached the upper clearing where the police had found Noel's belongings. They continued on to the lower clearing, where Noel said he had been attacked, and then found the location in the forest where Noel said he had found the documents. There wasn't much to be seen in any of these locations, but it helped to clarify what Noel was saying for the benefit of the officers. The three of them then walked back towards the helicopters and to the site where Noel had said that the stones had been left outside his tent. He found them quite easily, still in place, and he showed Inspector Olsson the photo on his camera which showed the stones in front of his tent.

The next step was to look for the remains of Noel's tent. It took a bit of finding, but eventually Noel led them to the correct location. It was a sorry sight. The charred bottle that had been thrown at the tent to set is alight was lying there, and Inspector Olsson picked it up and put it in a plastic bag to take with him for analysis, and as evidence. Noel felt encouraged by its discovery. Any thoughts that the police might have that he had set his tent on fire accidentally by himself, should now be out of the picture.

As they walked back to the helicopters, they heard one of them taking off, and saw it fly overhead, up the valley.

"Are they finished with investigating the body?" asked Noel.

"No, I think they are going to look and see if they can find anyone else. You said you thought there were at least three people involved?"

"Three or four I think. I hope they find the others."

Noel and Kristina were flown back to Gällivare. Back at the police station, Kristina said to Noel:

"I'm sorry, I can't allow you to go back to your hotel tonight."

"What, you're arresting me?"

"We can't understand how Mr. Elkins died, and we can't understand how you obtained the two documents. Hopefully by tomorrow morning we will have some evidence which establishes your innocence. But for now, I'm afraid, we need to keep you here."

"Have your officers looked in the riverbed to see if there are any of my footprints there? You have my boots, so you could recognise them," said Noel, not entirely concealing his anger at being detained.

"I thought you weren't wearing your boots after you were confronted, Noel?" It was an innocent mistake on Noel's part, but it didn't help his cause.

"OK, right, take my sandals, and see if they match any footprints, then," he said, curtly. He had left his sandals at the police station after being given the boots.

"OK, thank you for the suggestion, we will do that. But I am afraid that you will still need to stay here overnight. Also, one other

130

thing. We would like to download copies of all the photos that you took while on your hike, from both your phone and your camera. I have them here."

"OK, that's fine."

Kristina took Noel to a computer to download his photos and then took him, in a state of some anger and distress, down to a cell for the night.

*

Charles heard the distant sound of a helicopter from his and Thomas's hideout amongst the boulders. His heart sank, as he knew that it could very well be the authorities out searching for them. Maybe it was a reindeer herder, but when he saw that it was following their route to their hideout, presumably using their footprints in the snow, there seemed to be little doubt about it. The helicopter circled over the boulders where they were resting up, and they remained hidden. But the helicopter landed nearby, and two armed police officers got out, and walked directly towards them through the snow. It was senseless to try to run away. The officers arrested them both. They were soon on their way, in the helicopter, heading back to Gällivare.

*

When Kristina got back to her office she took up a line of enquiry that had only occurred to her to take while out in Rapadalen that day, but which she realised that, as soon as it did occur to her, was entirely obvious. She had a phone number for Sally Krosen on the authorisation letters. So she gave her a call.

"Hello," said Sally.

"Yes, I would like to speak to Sally Krosen, please" said Kristina.

"Speaking".

"Good evening. My Name is Kristina Lindberg. I am a police officer with the Swedish Police."

"Yes?" Sally knew that Matt was missing, and guessed that if the Swedish police were calling her it was something to do with that. But she had no idea how they might have got hold of her number, and was not keen to talk to them.

"I obtained your name from two documents which I have been given. One is called 'Covert Human Intelligence Source Authorisation' and the other..."

Sally was horrified. This police officer should never have been able to get hold of these documents. How had it happened? Had they arrested Matt?"

"If I can just stop you there. I am familiar with the nature of the document to which you are referring, and we do authorise covert intelligence sources. But I am afraid that we never comment on our operations. The safety and security of our agents is our top priority at all times."

"I would like to inform you that Mr. Matt Elkins, who is referred to in the documents, is dead."

Sally was taken aback. But she maintained her composure. "Well then that is something that you will need to inform the British Embassy in Stockholm of" she said. "I really can't help you. I'm sorry. Thank you for the call." Sally hung up. She had known that something was up, but still this wasn't at all what she wanted to hear. Would the Swedish police make these documents public? That could be a nightmare for her. The best thing for now was to say as little as possible.

If Sally was shocked, then Kristina was even more so. If the safety and security of the British government's agents was its top priority, then Sally seemed to have shown an appalling lack of concern that one of her agents was in fact dead. If this is what happened with the top priority, then how on earth did any secondary priorities work out?

Kristina phoned up the British Embassy in Stockholm, as Sally had suggested. They were not a lot of help. They were mostly concerned with the registration of the death, and notification to the next-of-kin. There was no meaningful conversation to be had regarding the covert operation carried out by Matt and his two accomplices.

## XIV

Tuesday 3<sup>rd</sup> October

The next morning Kristina brought Noel up to the interview room again.

"I have some photos of the body, which I would like to show you, please. You can tell me if you recognise him," she said.

"OK, I'll have a look."

Kristina brought an image up on her computer. It showed a man's face, in front of a plastic sheet. There were some wounds on the face. She clicked on through to some side views of the face.

"I don't know," said Noel, "I saw so little of him. It could be the man who was standing in the forest when I came down that night, but I can't be certain."

"OK, that's fine, thank you. We have difficulty understanding how Mr. Elkins died. Our experts have looked at the body. He didn't drown. He had some terrible injuries, a lot of broken bones, but not so much in the way of surface wounds. They say that it looks like he must have fallen from a great height to his death to have had such injuries. But how could he have fallen from such a height into the middle of the river? There are no cliffs by the river. We can only think he must have fallen somewhere and then an animal, or animals must have dragged him into the river. And he might have drifted down the river as well. But it's very strange."

Kristina had also discussed with her colleagues how Matt might have fallen. Might Noel have pushed him off a cliff, perhaps in a fight? The only cliffs that Noel had been near were on Nammásj and Låddebákte. The former was well downriver of where the body had been found, so there was no realistic way that the body could have come upstream from there. Noel had been close to a

134

lot of cliffs on Låddebákte, and his campsite there was close to one. But it would have taken a great deal for Matt's body to have been dragged from the bottom of one of these cliffs, and then carried down to the river to the location where it had been found. In addition, no footprints of any sort had been found in the sand around Matt's body, although admittedly they would have been hard to find through the snow.

What the police didn't know is that mountain demons have the power to lift a person up into the air as high as they like, before then letting him fall, back to earth, to his death. Dropping the person onto a sandbank in a river would be a good option if the demons wanted the body to be found. Maybe that is precisely what had happened to Matt.

"Yes, I just have no idea," said Noel, slowly shaking his head. "But you are certain that this person is Matt Elkins?"

"Yes, his face matches the photo on his passport which we found on him."

"Because Matt Elkins is the person who was authorised to spy on me. That means that somehow, somewhere I must have met him, and formed a relationship with him. Otherwise the criminal conduct authorisation wouldn't work. The meeting has to have been before he confronted me. So where did I meet him? I had thought that the man at the hut, Andreas, might be the person who was harassing me, because I did have some conversation with him before I set off on my hike. But this clearly isn't him. So I would really like to know how I met this person."

"In England perhaps, or on the train on the way up here?"

"I don't know."

"Well, if it does occur to you how you met him, then please let us know, we would be interested. Also, you will be interested to know that we picked up two more English people."

Noel sat wide-eyed. "OK."

"Our helicopter followed their tracks in the snow up a side valley off Rapadalen. They had walked a long way, almost to Norway. One is a man, one a boy, 15 years old. It sounds as if they could be the people who scared you up on the mountain."

"OK, well, well done."

"They are being questioned in the next rooms."

"You are free to go. But there is likely to be a court case against these two English. If you can be available to help us with that it will be appreciated. Of course, you are going to claim asylum, so you will be staying anyway?" she asked with a smile.

"Well, yes, I certainly don't feel that much desire to go back to England, right now. But I have to think about it."

"I'm not surprised, if your employer treats you like she does. Anyway, if you can please let us know where you are going to be."

"I will."

"I can give you your things back now." They left the interview room and Sally returned Noel's belongings to him.

"Oh, by the way, we got a translation of the words on the back of the document," she said.

"And?"

"We have a Sami police officer who is based in Kiruna, north of here. He looked at the writing for quite a long time, and then said that it means 'See schedule four bad crime law 2007'. We still don't know quite what that refers to."

"That is so strange! Did he have any suggestions as to who might have written it?"

"No. This is odd too. We asked him, and all he would say was 'Don't know. Maybe spirits.' They do believe in a lot of things, you know, these Sami."

## XV

Noel had a couple of days until his train left for Örebro. He decided to stay in and around Gällivare and not bring his train booking forward. There might be further discussions to be had with the police. Gällivare has an enormous iron-ore mine, which is really the main reason for the existence of such a sizeable town so far north. Noel was able to arrange a tour of the mine which he enjoyed, and which kept him occupied for the first day.

For the second day, Noel decided to go for a walk by himself on the hill known as Dundret, to the south of town. The hill is the site of a small ski resort, which would be due to come into operation in little more than a month. He took a bus out there, and walked up to the top. There was some snow up there already. While walking, Noel thought about what his plans should be now. While, at first, it had been a great relief for him to be away from his experiences in the mountains, he slowly came to realise that it did not necessarily mean that his troubles were over. If Sally Krosen had seen him as a threat to public order because of his plans to claim asylum, then presumably he was even more of a threat to the public order now. If and when it was revealed publicly what had happened to him in the mountains, there would be a huge outcry back in the UK, and massive protests. He would be in a position to reveal more information. So, if it had been necessary to authorise criminal conduct against him before, the case now was even stronger. Would she dig herself even further into the hole and authorise further operations against him? It was a real worry.

Noel realised that absolutely anyone he met now might be wishing to form a relationship with him in order to become a CHIS, and then go on to commit crimes against him. It wasn't a pleasant thing to have to worry about. It did weigh in favour of him staying in Sweden though – presumably it would be harder for the UK authorities to set up an operation against him in Sweden than it would be if he were back home, even if they had managed it once so far. He decided that, in any case, he would take his train to Örebro that night. There he would at least be able to explore the possibility of claiming asylum, whereas in Gällivare there wasn't that much for him to do. Also, winter was on its way in Gällivare and it was going to get very cold.

Noel went back to his hotel, called Kristina to let her know that he was heading off, collected his belongings, and caught the train. Once on the train, he further realised the predicament he was in. He was sharing his compartment with a Swedish man who was keen to strike up a conversation. Noel mentioned his hike, but didn't want to bring up any of the intimidation he had suffered. It was too much information. But could this man be a CHIS sent by the British government? How much of a conversation was necessary with the man such that a relationship would be formed, and a criminal conduct authorisation then come into effect? Would he again be mugged in the middle of the night? Would he find the stays on his sleeping berth released overnight, making him fall to the floor? He thought it unlikely, but still it was hard to get the idea out of his head. The ticket inspector came in. Was checking tickets enough to amount to a relationship such that the ticket inspector could now be a CHIS? The possibilities seemed to be endless.

In the event, the journey passed without incident, and, after a change of train north of Stockholm, Noel arrived at Örebro mid-morning. It was good to be somewhere with warmer weather and a more relaxed feel than Gällivare. Örebro, he felt, seemed more liveable, and more like a typical continental European city. He headed to his hotel and checked in. From his room he made a call to the Migration Agency and made an appointment to come in and see an officer there that same afternoon.

At the Migration Agency, Noel explained to a slightly incredulous officer his background in England, how he had had the idea of claiming asylum in Sweden, but had then been set upon in the mountains. He gave the officer Kristina's details so that he could check the story.

"If all of this is correct, then I can understand why you don't want to go back to England!" said the officer. "But it seems to me that your story is really more about what happened here in the mountains in Sweden, rather than your reasons why you felt you were persecuted back in England. I really think it will be hard for you to prove you were persecuted in England just because you are white and male. If your government was terrorising you in the way you said it was in this country then I am truly shocked. But you will understand that that in itself is not a ground for claiming asylum."

"I know."

"I can put in an asylum claim for you if you would like. But can I ask, how long will your existing funds allow you to live here in Sweden?"

"Maybe two months, I guess."

"OK, if you are definitely decided that you want to stay in Sweden then, you have 90 days on your visa anyway. I think you should look for a job. If you did get asylum it would be no different, you would still need to get a job eventually."

"OK. Do you have any suggestions? Maybe I could come and work here, given my background?" Noel asked, hopefully.

"No, I'm afraid I don't think it would work. You would have to speak Swedish for a start. But I can give you some other suggestions which I hope will be interesting to you." The officer got up and picked up two leaflets which he handed to Noel.

"These are what we often give to asylum seekers. One is details of a training course to become a software engineer. The other is for forestry work. I think you should look into both of those. Or in your case you could consider teaching English, I can give you details. If in a month you still think you want to claim asylum, come back and we will talk about it again. But if you have got a job then it should not be difficult for us to give you a residence permit without having to worry about asylum. I think that is simpler. How does that sound?"

Noel agreed that it was a sensible plan, thanked the officer, and headed back to his hotel.

## XVI

## In Örebro

Noel spent the weekend getting to know his way around Örebro. But he had some things that he wanted to do online, so he arranged some Internet access at his hotel, and spent some time on the computer there.

He had been thinking about how Matt Elkins could have formed a relationship with him in order to become a CHIS. He really could not recall anyone he had met who might have been Matt Elkins, certainly now that he had seen photos of him. But did the meeting have to be in person? Could it just be online? He had had a creeping realisation that there was a possibility that Tromso2000, who had been so helpful to him on HikeBackCountry.com might in fact have been Matt Elkins.

Noel logged in to HikeBackCountry.com. There had been no further posts in relation to his request for help on his hike since he left England. He checked Tromso2000's details, and saw that he had registered on the site just 40 minutes after he had posted his initial request, after which he had responded to Noel almost immediately. He had not made any other posts on the website. If Tromso2000 was Matt Elkins then that meant that (a) Noel had been being tracked online for Matt to have known so quickly that he had posted there, and (b) that Noel had told him almost everything about his hike, particularly his planned route. Noel felt physically sick at the idea that he might have inadvertently done so much to help the operation against him. He sent a message to Tromso2000 through the website, saying that he was back, and asking if Tromso2000 was still interested in hearing how it went. Would there be a reply?

The next thing that Noel wanted to do online was to look into the mysterious words written on the back of the documents. So he googled "schedule four bad crime law 2007", in accordance with the translation given by the Sami police officer. It was immediately apparent what this referred to – some UK legislation - Schedule 4 of the Serious Crime Act 2007. He looked over this schedule and could see that it related to the assistance or encouragement by someone, in the UK, of a crime abroad. This, in itself, was an offence under the Act. Of course! Sally Krosen's actions ought to be of concern to the police as well. She had authorised Matt's criminal conduct. So, supposedly under English law, that meant that Matt was innocent. But he could never have been innocent under Swedish law. So therefore, it looked as if Sally Krosen was guilty of having encouraged these acts in Sweden. But who on earth had helped him by writing those words? He decided for now just to accept the suggestion of the Sami police officer. If it was the spirits, then that was good enough. He had too much on his mind to consider who else it might be.

Finally, Noel scanned in the two authorisation letters signed by Sally Krosen, and emailed copies of them to her with the simple question "What are these documents?" He was due back at work on the Monday, but he didn't have a flight booked, and had no plans to be there. He would see how she responded.

On Sunday, Noel started looking for some longer-term accommodation in Örebro, and he signed up for the computer course. On Monday he phoned up Kristina and explained his suspicions about Matt having been the person he communicated with on HikeBackCountry.com. There had of course been no reply to his message to Tromso2000. He also explained what he had found out about the Serious Crimes Act. Kristina said that she was handing over the matter relating to Thomas and Charles to the public prosecutor, and that he would be in contact.

On Tuesday, Noel began his computer course. He was still troubled by concerns about the real identity of anyone he might meet. He had met lots of new people that day. Logically, any one of them could be an agent of the UK government seeking to form a relationship with him, to then go on to commit authorised criminal acts against him. He could see only one way out of this situation. And that was to reveal publicly everything that he knew, as soon as possible. And then make it clear that he was going to stay silent. Until such time as he had done that, it was going to be very hard for him to settle into his new life here in Sweden with the ever-present fear of a criminal conduct authorisation against him.

The next day, Noel had a phone conversation with the public prosecutor in Gällivare, to whom Kristina was handing over the matter. His name was Olof Dahlström. In relation to Charles and Thomas he explained that they would be appearing in court in two weeks' time charged with the crime of molestation in relation to Noel up on Låddebákte. Noel would be able to give evidence by video link.

"What about Sally Krosen?" asked Noel.

"Well, I saw that English law provision that you raised with Kristina Lindberg. I thought about seeking to have Ms. Krosen extradited here. But really her crimes were committed in England, and that is more the appropriate place for her to be prosecuted. So, if you agree, I would like to ask the police in England to investigate charging her under the law you told us about."

"Yes please."

"I will keep you informed."

"By the way, I have decided that I want to make everything that has happened to me public. I would like to set up a website and contact the press. I hope you don't mind me doing that."

"No, I don't think you should do that. Why don't you wait until any legal proceedings are finished? It is better if the judges don't feel that they are judging something that has already been judged by the public. And in your country you have trial by jury, don't you? If Ms. Krosen goes on trial under this law you have told us about, isn't there a danger the jury could be prejudiced by all the information you put on your website? I think better that you wait until all the legal proceedings have been dealt with."

"You don't understand my reasons," said Noel. He went on to explain his concerns about being the subject of further criminal conduct authorisations.

"I see. Quite a situation. Well, it is up to you. But still you must understand it could have consequences."

That afternoon, Noel had some more computer classes. He went out for drinks afterwards with a number of his classmates. There was a Swedish girl there, Ingrid, who hadn't been in the class the day before. He got on well with her, and ended up walking her home.

The next day, Thursday, back at computing school, Noel saw Ingrid again. He ended up having dinner with her. But once he got back home, the inevitable concerns started to build in his mind. What if Ingrid was another agent, sent by the British government, about to spring a criminal conduct authorisation into action at any time? She hadn't been in the class on the first day. Could this have been because it hadn't been possible to put an agent in place in time?

Noel was aware of cases in the past where (male) undercover police officers in the UK had entered into relationships, as covert human intelligence sources, with women. While the undercover operation continued, things had then progressed, beyond platonic relationships, to the point of marriage proposals, and the fathering of children, without the women in question having any idea of the real reasons why the men had entered their lives. When the undercover operations ended, the officers simply disappeared out of the lives of the women. In some cases the women later found out that the men had really been there to spy on them. This was of course extremely distressing for the women concerned. Noel was unlikely to be left holding a baby, but still, the prospect of getting involved with someone who turned out to be only interested in order to spy on him was very unsettling. He had not told Ingrid anything about the untoward events on his hike, but the time was approaching when he would have to, because Charles and Thomas's court appearances were due, and it would all become public. Just telling her wouldn't be enough though. She could express her sympathy, and still be an agent. The only solution was to get that website set up, make everything public, and then just get on with programming computers. If she were an agent then Noel would no longer be any sort of threat, and she would presumably lose interest.

Noel had no classes on Friday afternoon, and Ingrid was out of town until Sunday, having mentioned to Noel that she was visiting her parents. So he hired the office space with computer at his hotel, and got to work on his website. He registered it, www.noelmcvayhike.com, and worked solidly on it for five hours, explaining every detail of his story, and uploading photos and copies of the two letters of authorisation from Sally Krosen. He added statements that he would not be making any further comments until all legal proceedings were completed, he did not wish there to be any public disorder relating to the matter, and that he was now based in an unspecified location in Sweden. Once he was done, he emailed as many newspapers and human rights organisations in the UK as he could think of with a link to the website. He breathed a sigh of relief. He turned off the computer and went to the hotel bar where he sat down with a beer, and ordered himself some dinner.

When Noel woke up the next day he checked his emails on his phone – there had been no replies. He asked himself what he would do if nobody took an interest at all. But surely they would. There had been some articles in the Swedish press about Matt Elkins's death, so surely the press would get onto Noel's story before long. It was the weekend, after all. He went down for breakfast, and then returned to his room.

Noel checked his phone again. This time there was an email. It was from a human rights organisation in London that he had contacted the day before, by the name of Judicium. One of their lawyers, Anthony Worrald, who worked on a voluntary basis for the organisation, mostly at weekends, wanted to talk to him. Noel emailed back with his hotel's phone number and his room number and Anthony was soon on the phone.

"I have read over your website with great interest" said Anthony. "It's an astonishing story. We have had a lot of concerns for some time over the way criminal conduct authorisations are being used, and we are campaigning for them to be stopped. But normally the reports we have are just conjecture on our part, because we are never able to get hold of the authorisations themselves. You have been able to include copies of the authorisations. It's dynamite. If you are agreeable, I would like to put a short article on our website about your experiences with a link to your website."

"Sure. I want this to become public."

"But why, exactly? You may get a lot of unwelcome press attention through this."

"Because the logic that was used to attack me was that I was a threat to public order. If I can say everything that I have to say,

147

then I can cease to be a threat, and there should be no reason for a recurrence of what happened to me."

"I see. You are very bold, but I understand." Anthony asked for details of someone who could corroborate Noel's story, and Noel gave him Kristina's contact details.

"I understand. I'll speak to this Inspector Lindberg and, assuming I can do that, we should be able to publish something about your situation shortly. I'll also have a think about whether there is anything we can do to help you legally. Given that this Mr. Elkins is dead, and the Swedish police are on the case with regard to the others, I suspect there isn't much unfortunately. It seems that your boss acted within the law."

Noel then mentioned Schedule 4 of the Serious Crimes Act 2007 to Anthony, who said that he would have a look at it.

That morning and afternoon, Noel had more follow ups on his emails, mostly from the press. The journalists always wanted to ask him about his story, and at first he was happy to oblige. But then he remembered his plan to say everything on his website, and then just stop commenting. So he started replying to the effect that he intended to make no further comments on the matter, and he directed the journalists to Kristina Lindberg. Tiring of the phone calls, he took a break, to go for a swim in the hotel pool, and then had dinner in the hotel restaurant, as before.

The next day, Sunday, Noel had arranged to meet Ingrid for breakfast. He would forego the hotel breakfast, and meet her in the café at Örebro castle instead. They could then have a look around the castle. He did not check his phone before setting off to see what the press might have written about his story; he just wanted to enjoy his day not thinking about it, and really, he had said what he had to say to the press; it was out of his hands now. It was a beautiful day as he made his way on foot to the castle; he was getting a second dose of autumn now that he had come further south.

Noel arrived at the castle. It appeared grand, solidly built, and well situated, as it was, in the centre of town, surrounded by flowing water. He crossed the bridge and entered the castle through to the internal courtyard adjacent to which the café was situated. He went in. Ingrid was already there, seated at a table and she waved at him. He went over to greet her, ordered some breakfast, and then sat down to join her.

"Why is that man taking photos of us?" exclaimed Ingrid, all of a sudden, pointing at a man out in the courtyard. Noel turned around, and there was indeed a man taking photos of them. Ingrid waved him away, and remonstrated with him through the window in Swedish.

"Come on, let's move away from the window," said Noel, picking up his coffee and cutlery. "There's something I have to explain to you."

They found a table away from the window without a line of sight from the courtyard, and moved there.

"Go on then, please tell me," said Ingrid.

"Well you know I told you I had been hiking in Sarek before coming here?"

"Yes"

"Well, it didn't happen without incident."

"Meaning what?"

"Every night, when I was in my tent, people were appearing and trying to scare me."

"Really?"

"Yes. They threw things at my tent. They left mysterious rocks outside. One night a man just stood right outside, breathing heavily. And on the last night my tent got burnt, and I then got interrogated at knifepoint in the dark."

"Interrogated about what?" asked Ingrid, clearly rather incredulous about the whole story.

Noel would have preferred to avoid mentioning to Ingrid the fact that he had wanted to claim asylum. It would just make his story seem even more far-fetched than it already did. But having mentioned that he had been interrogated, he now had no choice.

"Well, please just bear with me on this. But I had some problems back home, and I had the idea of claiming asylum here."

"Right. So we sent a man from the migration office in the middle of the night to ask you about your asylum plans?"

"No. The man was British. He wanted to stop me from claiming asylum. In Britain there's an arrangement where, if you intend to do something that could lead to public disorder, the government can authorise criminal actions against you to try to prevent it."

"So you claiming asylum was going to create public disorder?"

"Yes, the government is struggling. There have been a lot of protests, and if I was to do something as extreme as claim asylum, there would be uproar. It would make the government look bad. England is supposed to be a country you claim asylum in, not from."

"I don't know whether to believe you or not." She was starting to seem quite cross. "And what's it got to do with a man taking photos of us anyway?"

Noel remembered the authorisations from Sallly Krosen which he had copies of. He didn't have the paper versions of them on him.

But he had uploaded copies to the website. He got his phone out and got the criminal conduct authorisation to show to Ingrid.

"Here, I got hold of the authorisation which was put in place for all of this. See this" he said, passing his phone to Ingrid. She read it over.

"What is this covert human intelligence source it refers to?" asked Ingrid.

"In order for them to set up a criminal authorisation against you, they have to authorise someone to enter into a covert relationship with you first. See here." Noel showed Ingrid the other document.

"And let me show you," said Noel, taking his phone back for a moment. "Here's a photo of my burnt-out tent. This is what they did."

"So all of this happened, and then you came down here to study computers?"

"I want to make a life here. I don't think I can ever go back to England now."

"Have you told the police?"

"Yes, the police in Gällivare are working on it now."

Ingrid closed the photo on Noel's phone, and saw that it was part of Noel's website. "So there's a whole website here about it?"

"Yes?"

"Did you put that together?"

"Yes, I did."

"You know, I'm not sure that I want to think about all of this right now. It seems like too much. Let's just finish breakfast, and then look around the castle as we planned. Then we'll talk about it later."

"OK, that's absolutely fine."

They finished breakfast, and headed up to the castle museum. The man in the courtyard who had been taking photos seemed to have moved on.

Both Ingrid and Noel were a bit too preoccupied by the conversation they had just had to really appreciate the various suits of armour and tapestries in the museum. Eventually Ingrid broke the silence.

"So that man who was photographing us, has he seen your website? Is that why he's interested in us?"

"Well I don't know if he's seen the website. He may have heard about it another way."

"Like what?"

"Maybe the press."

"So it's in the press as well?" Ingrid said, alarmed.

"I don't know, I haven't checked. It could well be by now if the press have seen the website."

"So I don't understand. Why did you produce this website? Did you <u>want</u> lots of attention from the press?"

Noel explained his concerns about being the subject of further criminal acts." Do you see my situation?" he asked.

"I suppose so."

"So it means that I can never relax until I get my story out. Anyone I meet might be spying on me. It makes life really difficult for me. It could be absolutely anyone. Even…" he trailed off.

"Even who, Noel?"

"Nothing, just forget it."

"Even who? Even ME? Is that what you're saying, Noel?"

"Well, anyone could be."

"Oh my word. Fine. If that's what you think, that I might be spying on you." She reflected in the idea, and concluded that it was so absurd that she didn't really care. "So do you want to keep going round the museum while I spy on you then, or not?" she finally said.

"I can't think of anyone I would rather have spying on me."

Ingrid laughed. "OK, let's carry on then. I'll see what I can discover."

The two of them carried on around the museum until they had seen enough. As they approached the exit, Noel was mindful that there might be more unwanted attention from the press outside. He took Ingrid's hand.

"You know, the next few weeks are going to be very difficult for me. If you can stand by me, it will be the best thing that anyone has ever done for me," he said. He didn't give Ingrid the chance to respond. He opened the front doors of the castle, and they emerged, still holding hands.

"Mr. McVay, can you confirm what is stated on your website?"

"Mr. McVay, do you have anything to add to what we have read? How long are you planning to stay in Sweden?"

Outside, there was a throng of press awaiting Noel, cameras and microphones at the ready, all shouting. The noise was intimidating. Ingrid was completely shocked by what she saw.

"Everything that I have to say is stated on my website," said Noel, "I have nothing to add. I am here in Örebro to do a computing course." He repeated this several times. He found it quite empowering to say it. Every time he could say it, publicly, he was emphasising that there was nothing that he might do, now, to threaten public order in the UK. After a short while, Ingrid and he fled to a taxi, which took them back to his hotel, where they went up to his room.

Inevitably, it wasn't long before the phone in Noel's room rang. It was a journalist asking for further details on the story. Noel repeated his now standard response:

"I confirm what is written on my website, but I have nothing further to add. I am remaining here in Sweden to learn computing."

Noel asked the hotel reception to tell any further callers that he had no further comments to make, and not to put them through. Ingrid looked on, still not sure what to make of it all. Noel turned on the television, and looked for a news channel. He also got onto the Internet on his phone. It was clear that his story was causing an uproar. There was discussion of it all over the Internet, and protests in England, including outside his workplace in Croydon. There was also footage of Ingrid and him coming out of the castle. He looked at her to try to gauge her reaction.

She looked back at Noel for quite a long time. Then finally, "I think this is rather exciting!" she said.

## XVII

The next morning, Monday, Noel called Olof Dahlström to ask him if he would speak with Anthony Worrald regarding the course of action to taken in relation to Sally Krosen. Olof duly gave Anthony a call. He ran over the situation, and explained that Charles and Thomas's trial was imminent.

"We don't like these sorts of things happening in our country," said Olof, "even if they are done by British people against British people. Elkins is dead. Routledge and his son are going on trial, but they didn't do all that much to be honest with you. But I think that Sally Krosen has blame in this. It seems it was her idea, and she authorised it and encouraged it all.  Sally Krosen's guilt in this is greater than that of the Routledges," said Olof, "I would like to seek her charged in England or extradited here for encouraging these crimes."

"Yes, I was thinking about that," replied Anthony, "but the problem you're going to have with extradition is that the courts will only extradite her if what she is charged with under Swedish law would have been a crime if committed in England. I don't know, but supposing what she did in England is a crime under Swedish law for which she can be tried in Sweden. Normally the question arises in extradition cases as to whether what was done would have been a crime if committed in England. But what Krosen did <u>was</u> committed in England. So the question remains, was what she did in England a crime under English law? And the answer must be no. Because the Regulation of Investigatory Powers Act makes it clear that the government can authorise crimes to be committed outside of the United Kingdom. So Elkins's actions were not criminal under English law. And therefore your Swedish law crime that you want to charge Krosen with could not have been a crime in England because there was no underlying offence in English law. So I don't think that extradition is a possibility, I'm afraid."

"OK fine. What about this thing then that Mr. McVay keeps going on about, the Serious Crimes Act 2007? Can she be charged in England with assisting and encouraging the crimes?"

"Yes, I find it quite impressive that he discovered that."

"Apparently, there was a reference to it written on the back of one of the authorisations, in Sami."

"A reindeer herder was out in the mountains and wrote down some helpful legal advice for him?"

"I don't know, we can't understand it either."

"OK, anyway. I think the answer is yes, she could be charged. When someone grants a criminal conduct authorisation for crimes in England, then those crimes are not crimes at all. That is what prevents the person from making the authorisation from being guilty of encouraging and assisting those crimes. But crimes committed in Sweden are still crimes under Swedish law – English law obviously can't prevent that. So the person making the authorisation is guilty of encouraging and assisting the Swedish law crimes. There seems to be no provision to save the authorising person from this."

"So we should ask the English police to prosecute this then?"

"Yes, I think so. I'm not sure what they'll say, but that should be our first step anyway."

"OK, are we going to approach them, or will you?"

"I would prefer it if you could do it, if you don't mind. We would very much prefer to keep a low profile. Otherwise, we risk fanning the current public disorder over this, and then you know how our government deals with that."

"With criminal conduct authorisations?"

"Exactly. We would rather not become the subject of one of them."

"OK, I will make a request through Interpol, and perhaps we can speak again later this week?"

"Certainly"

*

During the week, Noel and Ingrid attended their computing classes, while continuing to fend off the press. The protests in England continued, including, instances of bicycle attacks on government buildings. On the Thursday, Anthony received a call from Olof.

"I have heard back from your police," Olof said, "and they say that they will not prosecute Krosen. They say that the criminal conduct authorisation which she signed was valid, and it is not in the public interest to prosecute. I don't see how it can not be in the public interest to stop people from being terrorised when they go hiking. And also they have completely ignored our point about the Serious Crimes Act. It seems it is too subtle for them."

"Hmm, not altogether surprising, I suppose. There is an appeal process that Noel can follow, and I suggest he does. I'll send you details, and perhaps you can speak to him."

"OK, will do."

"However I fear the outcome will be much the same."

"Yes"

"There is another avenue that occurs to me here though. A bit off-the-wall, but perhaps it's worth thinking about."

"Go on."

"Well, you have a police force which understands all the facts in this matter. You are a prosecution service. What actually stops you from bringing a prosecution in the English courts?"

"We can't do that! It's outside of our jurisdiction. It would be for the British police to do that."

"Well, I did say it was unorthodox. But it could be done. It would be similar to someone bringing a private prosecution. If the British authorities aren't willing to help then it puts you in a stronger position. You will have the moral high ground"

"Maybe. I would have to give that a lot of thought before agreeing to it."

"For sure. There will be time for you to do so. Because I think that either way, Noel should appeal the police decision. If the appeal wins, then great, the British authorities can run the prosecution. If he fails then you look stronger in your decision to bring a private prosecution, because the police have shown that much more resistance. There would be difficulties with a private prosecution. Firstly, the Attorney General[2] will have to give his consent to the prosecution because of a provision in the Serious Crimes Act. And secondly, with a private prosecution there is always the possibility of the Director of Public Prosecutions taking it over and then discontinuing it. But in either case, I think the more you have shown that you are being reasonable in bringing a private prosecution, because the UK police have failed to act, the harder it will be for the authorities to hinder your prosecution."

---

[2] The principal legal adviser to the Crown and the Government in England and Wales

"OK, I'll think it over. If you want to send me the details for how Noel can appeal I'll speak to him about that first. Personally, I would quite like to see a criminal conduct authorisation against this Ms. Krosen. She seems to have been the biggest threat to public order in all of this."

Anthony laughed. "Yes, there would be some logic in it. But sadly we live in a country where the government can authorise crime against us, not the other way round."

"I know. OK, I will think about your suggestion, and I will call you back."

*

Charles and Thomas's trial came up, and Noel gave evidence by video link. They both pleaded guilty to molestation of Noel in relation to their actions up on Låddebákte. They were freed on account of time spent in custody while awaiting trial, and deported.

Noel's appeal against the police's decision not to prosecute Sally Krosen was refused, as expected. Olof spoke to some of his superiors about the rather extraordinary idea of the Swedish public prosecution service bringing a prosecution in England. They took some persuading, but after explaining the full situation, Olof had the all clear. He called Anthony back.

"OK, we would like to do this private prosecution. We have funds for it. I think It's the right thing to do in the circumstances" he said.

"Good. I think you will be making legal history."

"I have one concern at this stage, though. I believe we will need one of your barristers to present the case in court. Are you sure that any of them will want to take the case on? I mean, won't they be afraid of becoming the subject of criminal conduct authorisations themselves?"

"No, I don't think you need to be worried about that. They are expected to act fearlessly in the interests of their clients. And I think they will see it as a badge of honour to do so."

"That's good."

"One thing I should mention to you," said Anthony "is that you will have fewer powers in this than the British police would have. In particular you will have no right to get a warrant to search Krosen's office for any additional documents."

"That is a pity. But if your police won't prosecute I don't see what else we can do. But in any case, we have the two authorisations. They are strong evidence."

"Indeed."

The next day, Anthony instructed a barrister, Catrina Pell QC, who was very happy to take the case on. He and Olof then spent time preparing the case for her. Olof contacted the Attorney General, Amjad Hussain QC, for his consent to the prosecution. He refused, stating that it was not in the public interest. The use of CHISs and CCAs was an important tool in the government's fight against crime and disorder, and a prosecution of a civil servant for making such authorisations, on what seemed to be a technicality, would discourage further use of these tools.

The obvious response to the Attorney General's assertion was that the public was at that very moment holding protests against what Sally had done, so that the public, if asked, would undoubtedly consider the prosecution to be very much in its interests. On Anthony's advice, Olof pointed this out to Amjad Hussain. He decided to consult with another QC, David Sullivan, regarding the merits of the case. David Sullivan responded that he found the legal arguments in the case to be very weak. He said that, although the legislation did not specifically state that assisting and encouraging crime abroad was lawful for the benefit of the person authorising the criminal conduct, it must clearly have been the intention of Parliament in passing the legislation to make it so. There was a provision in the Regulation of Investigatory Powers Act stating that authorising criminal conduct abroad was permissible. Why on earth would that be there if it had been the intention of Parliament to leave the person making the authorisation in the lurch in this way?

Amjad Hussain agreed with David Sullivan. On the basis that the Swedish prosecutor's case was weak, and that a prosecution of Sally Krosen would do much to assuage the clear public anger over the affair, he relented. He notified Olof that he was providing his consent to the prosecution. The trial was on.

\*

Sally's trial was eagerly anticipated. The indictment charged her with intentionally encouraging or assisting assault, arson, theft and harassment to be carried out by Matt Elkins against Noel McVay in circumstances where (i) relevant behaviour of hers took place wholly in England and Wales, (ii) she knew that what she anticipated would take place outside England and Wales, and (iii) it was a crime where it took place. The facts of what she had done were fairly well established; she had signed the criminal conduct authorisation and lodged it, as required under the statute, with the Judicial Commissioner, so it was impossible for her to deny her involvement.

At the trial Catrina Pell presented the facts to the jury. David Sullivan was defending Sally Krosen. There was little argument about the facts, and the jury was already well aware of what had happened. The case then turned on the legal interpretation of the legislation. It was not a matter for the jury, so the judge, Sir

Stephen Donoghue, asked the prosecuting and defending counsel to address him in chambers.

"The issue here," said Sir Stephen "seems to be whether there is a gap in the legislation whereby Parliament has given individuals the power to authorise crimes, but failed to exempt those authorising individuals from criminal liability for encouraging and assisting the perpetrators in carrying out those crimes. This is only relevant where those crimes are crimes under foreign law. Ms. Pell, what is your position on that?"

"Your Honour, the legal situation is precisely as you describe it," replied Catrina Pell. "The defendant had the power to exempt Mr. Elkins from criminal liability, and the Regulation of Investigatory Powers Act duly contains a provision to put that exemption into effect. The draftsman of the Act understood that it was necessary to do so. But the draftsman made no provision to exempt the authoriser from criminal liability for assisting and encouraging crimes in circumstances carried out abroad. Had he been asked whether that is what he ought to have done, he might have said that it was. But he simply did not do it. The mechanism by which that might have been done is quite clearly not there. So the defendant is, assuming the facts to be as I have presented them, guilty as charged."

"Yes, I follow. Mr. Sullivan?" asked Sir Stephen.

"Your Honour, I have to respectfully disagree with my Learned Friend. it is necessary, as always, to look at the intention of Parliament when interpreting the legislation. It is simply unthinkable that Parliament would have seen fit to give individuals the power to authorise criminal acts while at the same time leaving them exposed to possible criminal proceedings themselves for assisting and encouraging those acts. The defendant had the power to make the authorisation. To try to tease out a distinction between authorising an act and encouraging or assisting it is totally contrived. It must undoubtedly have been the intention of Parliament to exempt individuals such as the defendant from criminal liability in making the authorisations which given them the power to do. That is how the legislation is to be interpreted. The defendant is innocent."

"Ms. Pell, do you have anything to add?"

"Yes, your Honour. I do not consider that the intention of Parliament is something that we can imagine exists in the same way as the intention of an individual in entering into a contract, for instance. Through debate and consideration in both chambers of Parliament, legislation comes into effect. It is a process by which laws are created. The relevant legislation is what that procedure creates. Nowhere in the legislation is there an exemption for crimes such as those for which the defendant is charged. It is entirely possible that, had members of both chambers considered it, they would have concluded that it was a desired provision. But if it was, it has simply not been put in place. The necessary mechanism has not been created."

"Mr. Sullivan, do you wish to add anything?"

"Your Honour I can only reiterate my view that the acts of encouragement and assistance are intrinsically bound up with the act of authorisation. Accordingly, Parliament has authorised them."

Sir Stephen instructed the court officer to adjourn the trial for the rest of the day, and retired to consider this important legal question. Although Catrina Pell had not mentioned it, he noted that the intention of Parliament could be said to be in existence even before an act became law. The intention could be deduced from draft legislation going through Parliament. What if Parliament intended to enact a law on a given date, but for whatever reason the date got pushed back? Might judges be asked to make rulings on the basis that the law in question was in force because it had been Parliament's intention for it to be so, even though in fact it was not? That didn't seem like good law. If he ruled that Sally Krosen could not be prosecuted, wouldn't he be setting a precedent for that sort of argument? The next day he addressed the court:

"Ladies and Gentlemen of the jury, I have heard legal arguments from counsel for the defence and for the prosecution in this matter. I have made my decision as to a question of legal significance in this matter, and I accept the view of counsel for the prosecution that these crimes are triable. Your role, as you know, is to consider the facts. If, on the basis of the evidence put before you, you consider beyond all reasonable doubt that the defendant did assist or encourage offences by Mr. Elkins as listed in the indictment, then you must convict her."

The jury retired, and didn't take long to reach its verdict. Sally Krosen was convicted of all charges. Sir Stephen sentenced her to three years' imprisonment.

Back in Sweden, having appeared in the proceedings by video link, and of course having closely followed them throughout, Noel heard the verdict. He took Ingrid out for dinner that night. It wasn't exactly a celebration; he did not really take pleasure in his former boss's downfall. But it did mark his relief that things seemed to be finally drawing to a close, and he felt vindicated. He could start to look forward to his new life in Sweden. The computer programming course was going well and he had a job offer at the end of it. And most of all, he was getting on rather well with Ingrid.

What of Stephen Kendale, and the issues with the ReachMe not working as expected? If the UK police had brought the prosecution instead of the Swedes, then they might have obtained a warrant, and discovered documents in Sally's files relating to Stephen's involvement. And he could no doubt have been prosecuted in the same manner as Sally. But it seemed that was not to be. Noel of course contacted Outdoor Tracking Services to make enquiries as to whether the ReachMe unit had been being used to track him, and why it seemed that his alarm had not gone through. But Outdoor Tracking Services were completely unaware that there might be such a problem. They said that they had had no other reports of a similar nature, and were ultimately unable to help. But Noel had published details of his concerns on his website. Based on that, the public's confidence in, and use of, the ReachMe, declined substantially. There were after all other devices which could be used instead. But Noel never really got to completely understand what had been going on with the ReachMe, and Stephen managed to find plenty of other things to occupy himself with at GCHQ.

## XVIII

### July, five years later

Noel had come back to Aktse for the first time since the incident. He now lived in a small town outside of Örebro from where he commuted into town to work as a software engineer. He had come back up north for a few days' break with Ingrid, to whom he was now married, and their three-year old daughter, Emma. They had no plans for any ambitious hikes of the nature that Noel had planned in Rapadalen on his previous visit. They would just have some family time, taking some short walks, and maybe a boat trip out into the delta. But Noel did have some unfinished business that he wanted to attend to. He set off one morning to repeat the walk that he had taken five years earlier along the base of Skierffe. At Aktse, he picked some flowers to take with him. As he walked through the forest, he picked up a reindeer's antler which he found, and carefully gathered some lichen from the trees. He reached the edge of the forest and carried on across the boulder field, as he had done before, until he got to the Sami ceremonial site. He had not forgotten his actions previously in throwing the three antlers out into the lake, and wished to atone for them.

Carefully, Noel laid down the antler he had carried onto the ceremonial rock, along with the flowers and lichen. He looked up towards the summit of Skierffe, clouds scudding across it in the wind, and stretched his arms upwards. He closed his eyes to take the moment in. And he offered silent prayers of thanks to the mountain spirits of Ähpár, for all that they had done for him, on that bleak night in Rapadalen, all those years before.

## Appendix

The Covert Human Intelligence Sources (Criminal Conduct) Act 2021 received royal assent and came into force in the UK on 1<sup>st</sup> March 2021. It inserted a new section into the Regulation of Investigatory Powers Act 2000, as follows:

"29B Covert human intelligence sources: criminal conduct authorisations

(1) Subject to the following provisions of this Part, the persons designated for the purposes of this section each have power to grant criminal conduct authorisations.

(2) A "criminal conduct authorisation" is an authorisation for criminal conduct in the course of, or otherwise in connection with, the conduct of a covert human intelligence source.

(3) A criminal conduct authorisation may only be granted in relation to a covert human intelligence source after, or at the same time as, an authorisation under section 29 which authorises the conduct or the use of the covert human intelligence source concerned.

(4) A person may not grant a criminal conduct authorisation unless the person believes—

> (a) that the authorisation is necessary on grounds falling within subsection (5);

> (b) that the authorised conduct is proportionate to what is sought to be achieved by that conduct; and

> (c) that arrangements exist that satisfy such requirements as may be imposed by order made by the Secretary of State.

(5) A criminal conduct authorisation is necessary on grounds falling within this subsection if it is necessary—

    (a) in the interests of national security;

    (b) for the purpose of preventing or detecting crime or of preventing disorder; or

    (c) in the interests of the economic well-being of the United Kingdom.

(6) In considering whether the requirements in subsection (4)(a) and (b) are satisfied, the person must take into account whether what is sought to be achieved by the authorised conduct could reasonably be achieved by other conduct which would not constitute crime.

(7) Subsection (6) is without prejudice to the need to take into account other matters so far as they are relevant (for example, the requirements of the Human Rights Act 1998).

(8) The conduct that is authorised by a criminal conduct authorisation is any conduct that—

    (a) is comprised in any activities—

        (i) which involve criminal conduct in the course of, or otherwise in connection with, the conduct of a covert human intelligence source, and

        (ii) are specified or described in the authorisation;

(b) consists in conduct by or in relation to the person who is so specified or described as the covert human intelligence source to whom the authorisation relates; and

(c) is carried out for the purposes of, or in connection with, the investigation or operation so specified or described.

(9) If an authorisation under section 29, which authorises the conduct or the use of a covert human intelligence source to whom a criminal conduct authorisation relates, ceases to have effect, the criminal conduct authorisation also ceases to have effect so far as it relates to that covert human intelligence source (but this is without prejudice to whether the criminal conduct authorisation continues to have effect so far as it relates to any other covert human intelligence source).

(10) The Secretary of State may by order—

(a) prohibit the authorisation under this section of any such conduct as may be described in the order; and

(b) impose requirements, in addition to those provided for by subsections (3) and (4) and sections 29C and 29D, that must be satisfied before an authorisation is granted under this section for any such conduct as may be so described."

The wording for the grounds on which criminal conduct can be authorised (subsection 5 above) is the same as that for the first three grounds for authorising a covert human information source, contained in The Regulation of Investigatory Powers Act 2000:

"s. 29 Authorisation of Covert Human Intelligence Sources.

...

(3) An authorisation is necessary on grounds falling within this subsection if it is necessary—

(a) in the interests of national security;

(b) for the purpose of preventing or detecting crime or of preventing disorder;

(c) in the interests of the economic well-being of the United Kingdom;

(d) in the interests of public safety;

(e) for the purpose of protecting public health;

(f) for the purpose of assessing or collecting any tax, duty, levy or other imposition, contribution or charge payable to a government department; or

(g) for any purpose (not falling within paragraphs (a) to (f)) which is specified for the purposes of this subsection by an order made by the Secretary of State."

Acknowledgements: With thanks to family members for reviewing the various drafts of this novel. Thanks also to Sweden for a most enjoyable couple of weeks which I spent hiking through the Sarek National Park during the Coronavirus pandemic in 2020, and obtaining ideas for this book. And thanks to the Swedish couple I met at Kvikkjokk Fjällstation at the end of that hike for the suggestion (in jest) that a British person might think of claiming asylum in their country.


My photos of the location of Noel's hike may be viewed at:
http://www.learnedtraveller.com/swedish-lapland-2019/sarek-2020/

Printed in Great Britain
by Amazon

71757721R00102